Cuffed for Pleasure

By JA Lafrance &
Michael S. Mann

Cuffed For Pleasure
Cuffed For Pleasure
Edited by: Julie Lafrance and Michael Mann
Formatted by: JA Lafrance
Published by: JA Lafrance & Michael Mann
Cover by: Julie Lafrance
Copyright © 2021 by JA Lafrance & Michael Mann

Blurb

Ryko "Spyder" Rymbersa is the owner of the most exclusive kink and fetish club, Temptation. A Master within the club and a single father outside the club.

Not everything is as it seems in Ryko's life. He wants to find a woman who not only craves the kind of kinks he does but falls in love with his son Tanner.

Larkin Pedience, a Shibari Mistress. She is hiding from a secret that may eventually find her.

She is tired of men who think she is weak or dumb and would love to find someone who challenges her.

Spyder sees his future in Larkin's eyes, but is he ready to give in to someone that is his equal?

Will Larkin's secret damage what she has fought hard to get over?

And can Larkin challenge Spyder's world and learn the true meaning of giving and taking.

Acknowledgment

We want to thank the readers for your patience as we bring you Spyder and Larkin's story.

We understand this is a cliffhanger, but we felt this story needed more time and love.

Prologue

Spyder

FIVE YEARS AGO.

"SPYDER, I CAN'T DO this shit anymore." Cadace waves her hand in the air as she cradles my son in her other arm haphazardly.

"What are you talking about, woman?" I growl as I watch my son slip from her grasp.

"You don't see all the women who throw themselves at you? It's like you are this gigantic pussy magnet, and you crave the attention!" Her screech startles the little bundle, and he begins to scream.

"For fuck sakes, Cadace, give me Tanner. You are going to drop him!" I yell as I step closer to her and Tanner, with my arms raised for her to hand over the tiny, precious bundle.

She tosses her head back and laughs as she throws him at me. I watch as she grabs his blanket in sheer horror, and he begins to unravel. I feel like everything is in slow motion as I dive to catch my son before he hits the floor.

"Awe, the poor baby," she sneers before she walks up the stairs and the door slams behind her.

I stumble a little as I bring Tanner to my chest. Before I can fall, I twist and land on my back, protecting my son's head as I land.

"I've got you, my boy. No woman will ever come between us, including the woman that gave birth to you." I let the tears fall before I sit up and reach for my phone. I dial the nine-one-one operator and fill them in on what just transpired.

As I hang up the phone, I stand with Tanner still cradled close to my chest.

It doesn't take long for the police to arrive at my door. I have a small bag already packed with my clothes and all the stuff I will need for Tanner.

"Officer Tan and Officer Rose, we are responding to a call of child endangerment and abuse. Is that the child in question?" He nods his head toward Tanner.

"Yes, sir, the woman who threw him is upstairs in the bedroom on the left. I am taking myself and my son to this address for his safety." I hand them over my business card before I continue. "Please come when you need to ask me any questions," I state and try to walk past. The petite female officer stands in front of me with her arms crossed and a scowl on her face.

"If you leave this house with that little boy, I will arrest you and make sure you go where she is going." She growls, but it comes out more like a purr.

"Officer Tan, I don't give a fuck if you think this is my fault. I have to protect my son, and being here when she is going to lose it, isn't protecting him. I gave you the address and my phone number. I'm not hiding anything. I just want to protect my son." I growl as Officer Rose looks at her, and she steps out of the way.

I walk out, ignoring the female officer's scowling face, softly singing a lullaby to Tanner. Almost immediately, he starts to fall asleep as I reach the SUV. I secure him into his car seat and softly close the door before looking back at the house. I should be upset that I am just walking away from something I worked so hard for.

A couple of seconds later, I see Cadace being dragged out of the house in handcuffs with the officers on either side of her as she kicks and screams at both of them, saying that she will make them suffer. Then she sees me standing by my car.

"Spyder! You are a dead man! You and that fucking spawn of yours! Do you hear me? You are both fucking dead!" Then she starts trying to run toward me, spitting everywhere as she lungs forward.

Officers Rose and Tan latch onto her and dig their heels into the lawn to hold her back. Tan tells Cadace to calm down and stop yelling when she twirls her head and headbutts Tan breaking her nose. Blood spraying all over Tan and Cadace did two things; it pissed Cadace off. Two, it causes Officer Tan to loosen her grip as Cadace takes advantage and starts running toward me.

Tan pulls out her stun gun and shoots Cadace in the back. As the electrical discharge drops her in her tracks, she lands face-first on the ground. Sobs and drool start dripping out of her mouth, but the fury in her eyes tells me that she will stay true to her word.

"Goodbye, Cadace," I state as I slide into the driver's seat and close the door. Pulling away from that hell, swearing that I would never return to her or the toxic relationship that we had.

"I promise, buddy, it will always be you and me against the world," I whisper while watching my son sleep in the review mirror.

Chapter One

Spyder

Today

I WALK SLOWLY INTO my bedroom, pulling off this noose or bow tie and the offending black jacket.

God, I hate getting all dressed up fancy for anything, but today was special, so I was willing to suffer the uncomfortable feeling of being in a tuxedo.

It's not often that your best friend gets married. You don't get to be the Best Man to the man who often gave you his blind loyalty.

After laying the tie and jacket on the bed, I walk over to the dresser, take off my watch, put it back in the fancy box that it came in, then place the box into one of the drawers in my watch case. I bought the watch and suit, especially for Tavis and Beth's wedding.

I wasn't planning on marrying again, not after dealing with Cadace and the divorce that took a grueling court battle to solve, but that was five years ago.

The memory of how I met her six years ago at the Club crosses the forefront of my mind.

That was how most of my clients became clients, and Cadace was no different. I smiled at that memory and the happiness I had in my life at that moment.

We made eye contact across the main floor and smiled at each other. Flirting with each other from across the room.

It only took a few seconds before she slammed her drink onto the table, then with a sway of her hips, she sashayed her way to me. Her well-manicured hand slithered up my chest when she reached me before pulling my head toward hers and running her tongue across my bottom lip.

We sat in the booth reserved for me and started to talk.

She ended up in my bed that night and stayed until she moved into my house a week later.

A month later, we were married, and a month after, we found out that she was pregnant with Tanner.

What was shocking was that she had been since our first night at the club.

At first, I wondered what had happened because I had used a condom that night. But she was happy about being a mom-to-be, but by the time Tanner was born, she had resented both of us. Stating that being pregnant ruined her body and that no woman should have to ruin a good thing to spend years of sleepless nights and no showers.

When the blowout at the house happened, it was a godsend. I had already planned to leave her anyway but wanted to ensure that Tanner was safe first.

With a shake of my head, life had been simpler back then. I had just started Club Temptation, and the opening had been a success.

Tavis, as always, had been one of the prime attractions that brought both men and women into the club.

Through their work, people eventually were able to find the sexual tastes they required and open up to find themselves.

Seems all my life, I have always gone against the norm. Society seemed to demand and want people to be themselves, both spiritually and physically. Still, if that included finding a particular sexual fetish that made them happy, society would cause a fuss. Everyone is supposed to be their own person. I get that if something goes against the norm, people tend to think it is wrong. But you can't judge someone by what turns them on. I mean, we all have specific kinks.

As I started walking away, I saw the picture of Tavis and Beth that I had placed on my dresser and picked it up with a smile.

It was about six months after the incident. They had been sitting at the patio table smiling and teasing each other, waiting for me to finish the steaks I had put on the grill. Beth's father, Chuck, had taken the picture and made sure that I got a copy.

That night was the happiest that I had seen them both for a while, and Beth seemed better than she had months earlier.

I talked to Tavis while flipping the steaks, and he said that Beth was doing good. I agreed with what he had said, but I knew better. It takes time to get over that kind of mental damage. Tavis had insisted that Beth's family was there at the dinner that night, and for a good reason. It was the night that Tavis officially proposed to Beth.

He got both Chuck and my blessings the week before. When Tavis acted like he had dropped something, he got down on one knee, waiting for Beth to see him, smiling like a fool while holding the ring box out.

When she finally did see Tavis on his knee with the ring, her jaw fell open as he asked her that all-important question, and I am sure that there was not a dry eye in the yard when she screamed yes.

It has been three years since all the Marcus Guidry shit happened to Tavis and Beth, and they both have grown stronger.

I put down the picture and finish stripping out of my suit to get it ready to go to the cleaners, then head to the bathroom for a quick shower.

Ten minutes later, I am in my regular office clothes and heading out the door to go to the club.

Starting my SUV, thinking about the day ahead of me. I have been trying to replace one of the club favorites specializing in Shibari-style bondage for months now.

The one candidate with the best qualifications was only available today for an interview. I had trouble replacing Tavis as the wax master at the club two years ago. Trying to replace the bondage master has proven to be ten times as hard. Rope masters are very specialized and don't like changing areas and building up new clientele.

This one was very willing to relocate to a new city and the club for work. Over the phone last week, she said that she wanted a fresh start and was willing to start at the bottom and work her way to the top. I started chuckling at that last thought I had. Starting at the bottom was an interesting phrase to say in this industry.

I pull into my parking spot at the club, turning my car off before heading to the back door and nodding at the security guard.

After Guidry was arrested, there were some vandalism and theft attempts, both to the property and to the vehicles, by members of his crew.

So Tavis and I set up extra security at all the entrances, with more cameras facing the parking lot and manned foot patrols around the building and through the parking lot. The extra security resulted in several arrests and many charges to Guidry.

After the trial, I had thought of getting rid of some of the extra security, but the positive feedback from the clients and employees had changed my mind.

They liked having the extra security. It made them feel safe. It also increased the clientele requesting to gain access to the club.

As I pass by Phil, he looks at his clipboard. "Boss, your interview is already here. I sent her to the main room to the reserved booth. She is waiting for you." A small smirk plays across his face.

"Thank you, Phil. Have Smyth escort her up to my office in ten minutes." He nods and quietly speaks into his radio. I scan my id card on the pad next to the door. The flash of green allows me to open the door and step inside. I turned to my left and headed up the stairs toward my office.

I quickly sat down and reviewed Ms. Larkin Pedience's file again. She has been an active member of the BDSM community in Las Vegas, working directly in the bondage field for five years. She became a Shibari rope master two years ago, working under the well-known Shibari Master, Master Lin.

It's not unheard of to be fast-tracked through training, but it is extremely rare that one can master everything being taught.

After reviewing the rest of her file and looking at the glowing letters of recommendation from her last employer and clients, it begins to make me wonder why she wanted to leave.

I flip through the file and find the pictures that she included. Looking at them again, one is of her in a leather outfit that crisscrossed her curvy body. She stood next to a St. Andrew Cross, with various restraints and ropes hanging next. In her hand, she held a flogger that matched her outfit. She was my walking wet dream.

Another image was of her in a professional dress. The tight bodice hugged every curve of her upper half, perfectly cupping her round breasts. The skirt was form-fitting and hit mid-thigh. An image that isn't supposed to be erotic, but her body was driving me nuts.

The final picture is of her in a two-piece swimsuit modeling on the beach. She has a body that men and women drool over.

She could have very easily been on one of those top model programs. The image of her posing brings up more questions that I need to ask.

Looking at the pictures again, I realized that she has different hair colors in all of them. She played a role and changed her look to fit every situation.

Flipping through the papers, I find her stats; age twenty-six, five foot five inches tall, strawberry blond hair, and lapis-colored eyes.

Looking at her eyes in the photo, they are a rich blue with purple highlights.

The mere sight of her eyes made my cock start to thicken. I have always chosen any woman I want, inside or outside of the Club. I always took full advantage of it, but she is different. The pull I felt from just looking at her pictures was new and different. I hadn't felt this way for a long time.

A knock at the door brings me back to reality. Quickly adjust my cock to not be too obvious when Ms. Pedience walks in.

Larkin's hands have a slight shake to them. I look into her eyes, and for a brief moment, I can see that she is nervous before a mask of confidence settles on her face.

Chapter Two

Larkin

"MS. PEDIENCE, IT'S nice to finally meet you. My name is Ryko, but everyone calls me Spyder. I own Club Temptation with my partner Tavis. He is currently away on his honeymoon with his beautiful wife, Beth. Please have a seat." He directs his hand to the gorgeous red leather high-back winged chair.

"Hello, Spyder. Please call me Larkin. Ms. Pedience is my mother, and that bitched died after she overdosed in front of me, blaming me for her death." I smile at him as his eyes widen, and he shakes his head.

"I see we have a similar past, only mine was a foster mother, and the reason she overdosed was that the father took a liking to men, yet she blamed me for him leaving." He reaches out his hand to shake mine.

"Thank you for taking the time to interview me for this position. I have heard nothing but amazing things about Club Temptation, and to have my name be associated with it will be amazing and a huge resume boost." I lower myself into the chair and push my legs to the side. My pencil skirt is leather and tight, so sitting any other way is highly uncomfortable.

"It says here that you have trained with Master Shin for your Shibari techniques, and you have developed your love of bondage through play. Can I please have you demonstrate your technique on me?" His question is one I was expecting, but as I sit and watch him take off his suit jacket and roll up the white sleeves on his dress shirt, my heart starts to pound. I have never reacted to someone like I am to him.

"Which rope would you like me to use? I have Jute and Hemp with me, or I can use your tie?" I pull out my beautiful royal blue jute and the tan hemp, placing them on his desk to allow him to choose which one.

"I'll use the hemp. I like a little more bite against my skin," he mutters.

I smile, thinking the rope isn't the only thing I would like to use to bite his skin. I'd love to sink my teeth into this man's skin and leave a mark on his body that lets other women know he is taken.

"Yeah, hemp does leave a little bite that some people love. I will use a single-column knot on your wrists. Please clasp your hands together like you're praying." I direct him as I pick up the rope and walk around his desk, pulling out his chair and turning him to face me.

I slowly wrapped the rope around his wrists and winded it up to his hands and arms before pulling the rope tighter to tie the knot.

As I finally get the right tightness, he lets out a hissed fuck, followed by a moan. I hadn't realized that I maneuvered myself between his tied arms and was sitting on his lap, rubbing my ass against the stiff erection in his pants.

"Shit, I am so sorry. I'll...just...get..." his scent is intoxicating, and the heat from his body against my back compared with the hard cock digging into my backside is something that I have craved forever since him. My ex-fiancée took his own life when he found out that he had lost his job. In his letter to me, he told me he couldn't go on not being able to accurately provide for me and that I needed to better myself. It's why I became a dominatrix with a focus on bondage.

"Fuck, Larkin, your ass feels amazing in my lap. I would love nothing more than to have you naked and taking my cock, but I promised myself I would never let another woman control how my life went." he groans as he leans forward and sucks the skin at my neck.

"I don't bend to anyone Mr. Spyder," I growl as I quickly undo the knot and take my rope off of him as quickly as possible.

"Larkin, I would love..." I hold up my hand and continue, "Let's continue this later. My email address and phone number are on the top of my application. If I am suitable for your club, please call me. I have another interview that I need to be at." I gather my things and head out the door.

Why do all men think I want them to bend me over and fuck me into next week?

"LARKIN," Spyder yells, but I am already out the door and heading to my car.

"Fucking stupid, Larkin. I can't believe you got close to that man. The last man you had was him, and he went away. He left you because he was selfish, but he was the first person in a long line of people to leave you." I growl at myself as I pull out of the parking lot and head toward my apartment. I don't have another interview, but I think it may be time to change careers. I need something to keep me alone and away from people, maybe like an Antarctica scientist.

Life has to get better at some point, right?

Chapter Three

Spyder

I WATCHED IN DISBELIEF as Larkin grabbed her ropes and bag and then rushed out of his office, "LARKIN!" I shouted, but she was already out of the room.

"Dammit, Ryko, you can be a huge dumbass sometimes," he watches the CCV monitors pointed at the parking lot, waiting for Larkin to get into her car before she starts the engine and drives off.

I try to stand up but feel weak in the knees, my raging hard-on drawing all the blood from one head to the other. What the hell was wrong with me?

After waiting a couple of minutes with my eyes closed, taking deep soothing breaths, and some mind-guided meditation, I can finally stand and get back to work.

I wanted to make sure that I had a clear mind to look at her resume again. But a simple flash of her modeling pictures makes the memories of what just happened come flooding back.

I knew she would be the perfect fit for the Club. Now I just had to figure out how to apologize for my actions and get her to accept my employment offer.

After getting Larkin's file back in order and some other mundane paperwork for the Club, I clean up my desk and put my jacket on. Looking at my wrists, I see the slight indentations still from the hemp rope. Smiling as I slowly rubbed my wrists, she made the bindings tight enough, just like I loved them.

Sighing deeply, I write down her address on my phone before putting it away. Maybe some flowers and a personal apology will help.

I wish I could ask Beth what to do, but there is no way I will interrupt their honeymoon for a stupid question about a mistake that I should be able to fix.

While heading out of the Club, I pass by Phil while scanning the parking lot, "Have a good afternoon, Boss, and have a good evening with your son."

"Thank you, Phil. You have a good evening," I say while digging my keys out of my pants pocket. I still had thirty minutes before picking up Tanner from his mom's.

Even though I have full custody of him and directly after the divorce, I wouldn't even let Cadace be in Tanner's life.

Her psychiatrist had asked that she have contact with him and the courts agreed. She agreed to have supervised visitations, thus allowing her to get to know Tanner and vice versa.

At first, the visits were rough on all of us, with him crying afterward, but Cadace and Tanner began accepting the situation after a few months.

At the end of two years of supervised visitations, she decided she wanted to be a mom again and have him in her life. So a long court session began with all three of us, including her psychiatrist. We agreed that she was allowed to have unsupervised visitations on alternating weekends.

That was about the time she ended up meeting Brennon. I admit that she has mellowed out a lot more over the last couple of years. Brennon keeps her calm and has ever since they got married.

However, what surprised me was that he had a couple of kids from a prior marriage himself that she took on as her own.

Brennon adores Tanner, so I was willing to let my child go over there whenever he wanted.

I pull out of the parking lot and onto the street, heading to their house, when a thought comes to my mind, causing me to chuckle; at least I haven't had to pay Cadace any alimony for a while now.

After twenty minutes of winding around the suburbs, I finally get to Brennon and Cadace's house, slowly pulling into the driveway and shutting off the engine.

I sit there for a brief minute, looking at everyone through the big picture window. Tanner is chasing the other kids around the room while Cadace and Brennon sit on the couch laughing at all the commotion my son is causing. They all had smiles on their faces and were having fun being a family.

I enjoy the life and family I have with my son. There are several members at the Club that I have proven their loyalty to me and have become my close friends.

Tavis and Beth have become the only family as important as Tanner, but with them getting married and watching Cadace and Brennon, it makes me realize that I am lonely. The parade of women who come into the Club and my bed aren't enough anymore.

Cadace was right when she said that I was a pussy magnet. I've always known that women are drawn to my looks, even as a teenager. Yes, I haven't been bothered by the endless parade of pussy that struts in front of me.

Having the bad boy reputation allowed me to be a picky manwhore. My reputation has helped to bring in some top female clientele.

Several years later, paired with the fact that I am getting ready to turn forty-five in a couple of weeks, it has become too much for this bachelor.

I get out of the SUV and walk slowly to the front door, stopping for a couple of seconds, trying to control my breathing. I smiled before ringing the doorbell.

The door snaps open, and Brennon's kids run out, grabbing onto each of my arms, "Uncle Spyder!" Both girls squeal as they hug me tightly.

I look down at the girl on my left arm and smile, "Hi Myrna, you have grown since I saw you last week. What are you now, twenty years old and almost six foot?" Myrna giggles and punches me in the arm.

"I'm only thirteen, silly! I did grow some, though. I'm at five feet even now!" I turn and look at her sister Mystie who has a death grip on my right arm.

"So that makes you the smaller older sister?" I try to say with a straight face, but the huge grin that spreads across my lips gives it away. Mystie giggles and punches me in that arm. "You know I'm thirteen years four minutes older, and I am still taller than her. I'm five foot one, thank you very much."

I tighten up my arms and then lift both girls off the ground walking into the house with twin squeals bouncing off the walls as they hold on for dear life.

"Well, I stand corrected then. Not sure how I got two of my favorite girls' ages so wrong. I guess you will see me with a cane next time." I chuckle.

The girls let go of my arms and pulled me down. I squat low enough to give each one a chance to kiss me on the cheek.

"You are not old Uncle Spyder!" Chirps Mystie and Myrna, at the same time, then run into the family room to get Tanner. Cadace walks into the foyer, smiling at what happened.

"Those girls love you to death, Spyder. They love Tanner too."

"I love them as well. You are doing a great job raising them, Cadace. I don't tell you that very often, and I should. You're doing a great job with all the kids. Thank you for making me see that you have changed."

Cadace narrows her eyes and looks up at me softly. She asks, "Are you okay, Ryko? You seem off today. Anything weird happened at the wedding?"

I shake my head, "No, Cad, the wedding went great, and they are off to Niagara Falls as we speak." I sit down on the bench and look at Cadace, "Do you think we could have worked things out, or we could have gone in a different direction?"

Cadace comes and sits down next to me, taking my hand in hers," Ryko, we both were young and naive about the world. Yes, I hated you when you called the cops on me that day, and forgive me," lowering her voice to a barely audible whisper, "I hated Tanner as well because I all I could focus on was my hatred of you." She lifts a hand to my face and cups my cheek.

"You had every right to do what you did to ensure our son's life was safe, and I do not hold that against you. No, we would not have been able to work things out and be together. Some people cannot be together as a couple, including us. We were supposed to be together to have Tanner and then move on. I have a wonderful husband and, two beautiful girls, one precious little boy, and I have you to thank for that. You are a great father, a great Uncle, and an amazing friend. Thank you for being you."

I smile and look into her eyes. The happiness radiates from them, "Thank you, I needed to hear that today. I wasn't kidding when I told the girls that I was getting old and today made me feel that way more than normal. Maybe it's time for me to settle down and find someone."

Cadace tilts her head back and gives me a weird smile, laugh-type thing before placing her hand over her heart and saying, "You! The great Ryko 'Spyder' Rymbersa, the master of Club Temptation, wants to settle for one woman and do the family dream? Now I've heard everything."

I stand up as Tanner comes running into the foyer," Daddy! Love you!"

I scoop him up into my arms and hug him tight as I look at Cadace, Brennon, and the girls who had come in behind Tanner holding his backpack. I took the bag from the girls and shook Brennon's hand, "Thank you" was all I said to him as he nodded back. The girls open the door for me as I walk out to the porch. I pause, looking at Tanner, "Everyone deserves a second chance at happiness. I like to think so anyway."

"Yes, Spyder, you deserve a second chance to find happiness. Of all the people that I know, you are the one that deserves to find it the most.", Cadace states before I hear the door close softly.

"Yes, I agree, and it is time that I start looking," I said to Tanner, who gave me a puzzled look that only a six-year-old can give, then hugged me again as we got into the car.

I decided to stop at a local flower shop on the way home. Tanner's eyes grew wide at what the shop had to offer, and he started looking at all the flowers in every color that could be imagined. The shop owner smiles at Tanner and hands him a balloon, grinning like he was just handed a million dollars. The owner then looks at me, "I am Mr. Moom. Now that the little master is happy, what can I do for the owner of Club Temptation?"

"I fuc... messed up with someone, and I need to give her something that says that I am sorry, that I was a dummy, and come back to me." Mr. Moom smiled, "Girlfriend trouble?"

"No, this is a potential hire for the Club, and my part of the interview went so terribly wrong. I want to smooth things over and have her work for me. Do you have anything that says that?"

"Why yes, I can make something for you to get back on her good side and hopefully help her say yes to the job."

"Thank you, Mr. Moom. Cost is not important. Just do your best." Mr. Moom smiles and waves me to a nearby chair.

"Please take a seat, and I will perform some magic for you. Fill out the card that will be included, and I will be right back." He hands me a card with an envelope and then walks into the back.

"What should I say to her? That Daddy messed?"

"Daddy," Tanner sings.

"You got this, dude!" He smiles and then starts to giggle.

"Where did you learn that!" I question my son.

"The girls," He shrugs. "I think they got it from a TV show." I shake my head and go back to writing the card.

Larkin,

I would like to apologize for what happened and want you to come work for me at Club Temptation as Headmistress. You will make a great addition to the Club, and I look forward to seeing you there. I promise to be on my best behavior.

Sincerely, Ryko.

I place it in the envelope, running my tongue along the edge to seal it. As I place it on the counter along with Larkin's address, Mr. Moom walks out of the back with a large bouquet of various flowers in a crystal vase.

"Will this do?" He asks as I look over the selection.

"Yes, I think it will be what is needed to smooth over my mistake. Here is the card and her address. Can you deliver it tonight?"

"Yes, sir, I can make sure it is delivered promptly. Please let me know if she likes it and if she starts working for you. Call it customer feedback for services rendered."

I pull my wallet out and put three one-hundred-dollar bills on the counter next to the envelope.

"I know that this is more than what you will be charging me. The tip is included for the delivery. Thank you, Mr. Moom, for helping me out of this sticky situation."

"Alright, Lil man, time to go home and eat. What do you want for dinner tonight?"

He takes my hand and starts toward the door. "Hot dogs and pizza!" Mr. Moom chuckles at Tanner's answer as we walk out of the shop.

"How about pizza tonight and hot dogs tomorrow." My ever-resourceful son looks up at me.

"Only if you are buying." I snort out loud at his answer and pick him up.

"Deal, dude! Let's go home."

Chapter Four

Larkin

"THE NERVE OF THAT MAN, thinking that it was okay. Thinking I would be the one to bend to his will." I mumble to myself as I walk into my house and slam the front door.

I toss my purse across the room, watching with pure satisfaction as it hits the corner of the table and, in slow motion, flips and opens spilling the contents onto the floor.

"Now, that's funny." I burst out in hysterical laughter as my little dachshund, Dick, comes shuffling into the room.

I walk over to the dining room table and turn on my laptop. After my blow-up at Ryko, I'm not holding my breath that my interview went well with Club Temptation. I honestly don't know why I freaked. Normally, any man who tries to dominate me gets easily put in their place, but Spyder. Yeah, he hit something deep in me that only one other man had, and that man tried to kill me.

When Spyder had turned the tables on me, I knew then that I would have said yes, that I would have made sure to please him in any way I could. The end game would have been my submission, and I can't let another man take that from me.

I plop down on the couch and kick my feet up onto the table and close my eyes, flashing back to the memory of meeting Nick and how fast he went from romance and flowers to anger and knives.

Walking into the Club Destination with JJ, he offers his hand to me as I place my overcoat and small purse in it. I notice a tall, muscular man with long blonde hair up in a bun. His body faces the stage, and his head is turned to the side, talking to the petite bartender Mina.

"JJ, who is that with Mina?" JJ's head snaps around and narrows on the bartender, who nods and turns to stop in her tracks. As her head slowly turns to us and connects with JJ's glare, her head lowers, and she quickly walks toward the bar.

"Why did you do that?" I smack him in the arm as I head toward her.

"Good evening, Lark. How are you today?" She smiles at me before quickly lowering her head.

"My brother is a jerk face. I am sorry he is acting like that." I giggle as she shakes her head.

"No, No, Master Jace has every right to be mad. I was looking at Sir Nick, and I am supposed to keep my head down. I have earned the punishment that he will give me." A small smile perks her lips as she slowly raises her head and looks at me. She must have caught something over my shoulder because suddenly, her back snaps straight, and her eyes narrow before she turns around, leaves behind the bar, and continues right out of the club.

I spin around and notice JJ gazing into a sub's face, his hand on her face as he looks at her.

Jumping off the stool, I stomp over and stand behind the chick. "Club Destination rule number ten, If a Dom has claimed a sub, they are to be committed to that sub and that sub alone, and vice versa. So big brother, while you get mad at Mina for doing her job, you should be fined for not doing yours."

His head snaps up, and then he quickly drops his hand before looking over his shoulder at the empty bar.

"Where is she?" I smirk at him and spin toward the bondage area, with JJ demanding I tell him where she is.

"Whoa, their pretty girl, what has you stomping around?" A deep voice states from behind me.

I spin around and look into the eyes of Sir Nick, a man that captivated my attention.

I lower my head, "Sorry, sir, my brother broke a rule, and it upset me. I came here to watch the shibari demonstration as it always calms me down."

He brings his finger to my chin, "whatever calms the beast is my thoughts. Have you ever been part of a shibari lesson?" I shake my head.

"Will you be my test subject?"

That was the first time I was introduced to shibari and the romantic side of Nick. After that, it seemed to have gone downhill.

If we were at the club, his bindings got tighter. The marks became deeper and stayed longer until it wasn't pleasurable.

I take a deep breath and close my eyes as the tears fall.

"Nick, please stop," I begged him as his hands gripped my neck tighter.

"No," is all he said as his free hand gripped the cattle prod and pushed it into my thigh.

"Please, you're hurting me," I whisper as the air gets harder to get.

"Too fucking bad. I warned you not to tell your brother what happened. I told you that it was an accident. But you couldn't keep your mouth shut!" Spit lands on my cheek as the prod is moved further up my thigh. I know that he plans on marking my pussy. I just don't know-how.

He throws me to the bed, gripping one ankle and tying it to the corner and doing the same to the other. My hands are still cuffed, and he hooks them to the bed.

The prod makes contact with the skin at my inner thigh, and as I begin to scream, the smell of burnt flesh starts to fill the room.

"Please, stop." I plead as tears stream down my face.

My body is on fire, literally. The pain is starting to make me numb until Nick turns the instrument on the outer lips of my pussy. The pain, the crying is all it takes for me to pass out.

I remember waking up in the hospital with JJ beside me, crying, and the police standing at the door.

That was when I decided to leave, and I never looked back. JJ knows where I am, but he is the only one. Not even my parents know that I live in a town forty-five minutes from them.

My doorbell chimes, and as I raise to get it, Dick decides to let the person know that he is guarding me.

"Down Dick, we all know that you bite ankles." I giggled as I opened the door to a beautiful bouquet of mixed flowers.

"Delivery for Ms. Larkin Pedience," the older man says with a huge smile.

"That's me, sir." I smile as he hands me the card.

"Go on and open that," he says as he holds the bouquet.

I open the card and read it aloud:

Larkin,

I would like to apologize for what happened and want you to come work for me at Club Temptation as Headmistress. You will make a great addition to the Club, and I look forward to seeing you there. I promise to be on my best behavior.

Sincerely, Ryko.

"No wonder he was out of sorts. Congratulations on the job. I wish you much success." The man smiled at me and placed the bouquet in my hands before turning around and heading back to his truck.

"Well, that's a first. It's not every day you get offered a position with flowers." I chuckle and walk toward the kitchen.

I guess I don't have to look for a job after all.

Chapter Five

Spyder

WHEN THE ALARM GOES off at five in the morning, I swing out of bed and sit on the edge for a couple of minutes, stretching and slowly waking my mind up.

I think about the night before and how great it went with Tanner after we got home.

As promised, we had pizza for dinner, but not store-bought. He ended up talking me into making homemade pizza while in the car.

Even though I half-heartedly tried to say no to making pizza, the thought of it sounded fantastic, and Tanner always loves to help me in the kitchen.

An hour after we got home, we had destroyed the kitchen making the pizza and placing it in the oven to cook.

That is one thing that I have always been surprised about with Tanner. He always wants to make sure the house is clean and organized.

His room is always clean, and all of his toys and books are put away in what he said was their proper home.

Once the pizza has finished cooking, we grab some slices and our drinks before going to the family room to eat and watch a kids' movie. We picked out this particular movie this morning. Some live-action remake that had a blue genie in it.

After the movie ended, Tanner went upstairs to take a bath while I cleaned up and put the leftovers away before packing our lunches for tomorrow.

Nothing like pizza the next day to make the world a better place. I help him get into his jammies, then tuck him in.

I grab the book that we had been reading together, but as I turn around after getting the book, I see that Tanner is already asleep and gently snoring.

Chuckling, I put the book back in its home and quietly leave his room before heading to mine.

Normally I would work out in my basement gym for an hour, but it had been a long day.

After sliding into my bed and checking my phone, I see a couple from the club about having to kick a few drunks out for causing problems with the female servers.

Shaking my head, I text back that I will review the video when I get to the club in the morning to see if a permanent ban was needed.

Opening my emails, I see that Larkin had not sent anything saying that she was taking the job or saying thank you for the flowers.

Feeling a little disappointed, I put my phone down and got comfortable. In no time, my eyes have grown heavy enough, and sleep takes over.

* * *

I rub my eyes and yawn, stretching as I stand up, wondering what kind of day it is going to be.

Frowning at that thought, I grab my phone and head into the bathroom. I take off my sleep shorts and look at myself in the mirror.

* * *

"Ryko, none of that negative bullshit from your mouth!" I tell myself as I poke my mirror self in the chest.

"No matter what happens today, you will have an excellent day because you will do your best and be your best!"

I look at the messages and see that Larkin sent me a text earlier. My eyes grew before I smiled as I opened the text and read it.

Larkin: Good morning, Ryko. I just wanted to thank you for the flowers and the position at the club. I will accept the position and be there this morning to start the paperwork. I wondered what outfit I should wear today as it is my first day. I want to look like a professional but not overdo it, and I don't think walking in wearing my dominatrix outfit would be quite right, although the business world does say to dress like you are starting to work right then. Anyway, I hope you had a wonderful evening last night, and I look forward to seeing you and the rest of my co-workers today.

The photograph of Larkin in her Domme outfit flashes through my head and makes my cock twitch. The reel of Larkin images begins to play behind my eyes, her in the bikini, and then the skintight dress and the memory of her grinding that perfect ass into my cock, has my dick so hard that I could hammer a nail.

I text her back, thanking her for accepting the job and saying that the HR department opens up at nine. I informed her that business attire needs to show a professional front but asked her to bring some casual business clothing.

Tossing the phone on the counter and rushing through the shower, making sure to turn the water to cold to try and calm down my raging erection, it has a mind of its own and pulses as the water cascades over it.

Switching the water too hot, I grab the body wash and squirt a bunch into my hand, lathering up my cock, running my hand slowly up and down the ridged shaft before closing my eyes and slowly stroking while imaging Larkin was tying me up to the cross and using her flogger on me.

Moaning deeply, my stroking becomes harder and faster while letting my imagination run wild. Thoughts of her whipping me on every exposed part of my body while smiling before caressing my hard cock with her sharp nails has my mental image forcing the cum to shoot hard across the shower hitting the glass door.

The sheer force of my orgasm caused me to get light-headed and weak in the knees.

Chuckling softly, I lean against the wall and let the water cascade over me while trying to catch my breath while slowly jacking off some more, wishing that Larkin was there in the shower.

Feeling myself starting to get hard again, I smile before humming the theme song from a cheesy sci-fi show while I finished up in the shower.

Cringing at the stains I left on the glass door. I wash off my cum from the door so that the housekeeper won't freak out.

Stepping out of the shower and grabbing the towel off the rack, I start drying off while heading to the closet to get dressed.

Passing Tanner's room, I knocked on the door before opening it slightly and telling him it was time to get up.

"Dad, I'm downstairs already!" His soft voice comes from the kitchen.

Wondering why he is up already, I hurry down the stairs expecting to see something wrong. Instead, he is up fixing breakfast for us.

"Morning Dad. I fixed you some cereal and fruit this morning. I hope you like it." I look toward my six-year-old sitting at the table and the bowl of fruity rings and a plate of sliced bananas at each of our chairs.

"It's perfect, buddy. Let's eat." I sit down, and after doing our morning ritual of clinking our silverware together, we dig into our meal.

Thirty minutes later, we walk out of the front door and get into the SUV. Chatting about our normal morning stuff as I drive both of us to his school.

Reminding him that his nanny would be picking him up after school as I have to show my new hire around the club.

"The one you messed up with will be working for you?" He asks as he adjusts his backpack on his lap.

Smiling as I glance at Tanner in the rearview mirror, "yes, sir, she texted me this morning that she was taking the job, so I guess she forgave me."

"That's cool, Dad. I'm glad she did. She makes you happy," he states while looking out the window.

I think about what happened earlier this morning, how her text sent my body into an internal flame that led to playtime in the shower. Tanner saw that Larkin made me happy.

"She did make me happy by taking the job. Just like you made me happy by making breakfast this morning. Today will be a great day." I slow down and pull into the school drop-off line.

Tanner jumps out, and we say our byes. I inform the teacher on duty about the nanny picking up Tanner before pulling forward.

Twenty minutes later, I pull into the club and park in my assigned spot, sitting for a few minutes with my eyes closed while the song on the radio finishes up.

Feeling that today will have new meaning and set me on a new path. Having Larkin working for me, a couple of things occurred to me. I do have feelings for Larkin. I know that I will be claiming Larkin, and two, I will do it my way.

Chapter Six

Larkin

"LARKIN, YOU KNOW I would have given you a job here." My Papa says as he starts coughing.

"Pops, are you taking care of yourself?" I unwind the curling iron from my hair before spraying some heat treatment onto the next strand and twisting it.

"Yes, sweetheart, I'm just getting over a cold. Nan made sure I was on the mend before she went on her trip." I sigh, my Nan always goes on one trio a year, and I know how hard it was for her to leave Pops.

"Papa, you know I had to leave. If I stayed, he might have killed me." I whisper.

"I know, sweetheart, your Nan and I will be up to check on you in a few weeks. Make sure you tell Ryko that you're my Granddaughter. He will treat you right. I will talk to you in a few. Love you, Princess." With that, he hangs up the phone.

Having to tell Ryko not only who my grandfather is but also that the man who tried to kill me is also the man that my parents sold me to pay off some debt will be the worst part.

The man that I was sold to, the man that is known worldwide for slowly torturing innocent men and women just so that they remember his name, none other than Rafael Restrepo, better known as Repo. Only he doesn't repo cars. No, he repos your family and forces them to work for them in ways that always make him a model citizen. I was supposed to be his side piece. The one his wife knew about. The one his wife was supposed to be happy with until he became obsessed with me.

I remember the night I finally got away. He had just finished inside of me when she walked in fuming. She demanded that he kill the thing that was living inside me even though I wasn't pregnant. To appease her, he stabbed me in the abdomen and then escorted her out of the room when the blood became too much.

His right-hand man came in after, and after seeing all the blood on the floor, he rushed me out of the room. He had been the one to call my grandfather when he got me across the border and into a hospital. The doctors and nurses rushed to save my life, but they had to give me a complete Hysterectomy to save me, or else I wouldn't be here today.

My alarm goes off on my phone, kicking the memory of that night out of my mind and bringing me back into focus on what I had to do today.

I had to be at Temptation in thirty minutes, and I was still standing in front of the mirror in my leather bra and pantie set, with my thigh-high leather boots.

Standing in front of my bed, I wonder which outfit I should wear. One has a leather skirt with a corset and cropped blouse. The other has a pencil skirt with a flowing top.

I decided that I needed to fit the part, so I put on the leather and left the bedroom.

The drive to Temptation was peaceful. I listened to the local radio station and decided that it needed to be part of my routine moving forward.

Pulling into the lot, I notice a sign on the spot at the front, 'Reserved for Madame Larkin'. Smiling as I glide my car into the spot, I pause briefly, remembering I need to be upfront with Spyder.

"It's now or never, Larkin, go in and tell him your grandfather is Capo Caladria," I whisper before opening my door and sliding out. I walk confidently to the building and head straight for the main office, pausing at the door, taking a deep breath, and knocking.

"Come in." Spyder's voice can barely be heard through the thick oak door.

"Holy fuck," he mumbles as his eyes roam over my body. He stands up and stalks around the desk, a low growl coming from his mouth.

"Shut the door," His voice is low. I spin around and quietly close the door.

"Stay like that and listen, do you understand?" He speaks, sparking a flood of arousal from my body.

"Words!" he barks.

"Yes, Master Ryko." I purr. What the hell is wrong with me? I am usually the one in charge. I have never had the urge to submit to anyone, but Ryko is different.

"Red means stop. Once you use the safe word, I stop, and I will not touch you. You are safe with me, understand?" He steps up to my back and runs his hand across my leather-clad ass.

"Yes, Master Ryko." I purr.

"I want you to slowly spin around, and pull your skirt up, show me what you have on underneath." I hear a zipper before I slowly turn around, making eye contact with him and gently wiggling my hips as the skirt slides up my thighs and bunches at my waist.

He hisses, and as I lower my eyes, I watch his hand leisurely stroke up and down his naked cock. I begin to reach out when he growls.

"No touching. I want you to lean back and run your hand over the outside of those sexy as fuck leather panties. I want to watch you cum."

Leaning back, I spread my legs and began to rub my needed cunt. As soon as my fingers press on the leather part, the sparks burst, gliding my hand up and down, bringing the pleasure rolling through my body.

"I want you to cum, Larkin, moan for me, scream my name to the world. Do it, do it now!" He growls as my head hits the door, my legs start to shake, and the orgasm takes over my body.

"Fuck Ryko, that feels so good," I scream.

Suddenly, my hand moves, and I can feel warm, hard skin being pushed between my pussy lips and panties. He begins to move his body erratically before he groans low in his throat, and his cum fills my panties and the swollen wet lips of my pussy.

He pulls out and cups the warmth between my legs, "You may be the Dominatrix of Temptation, but you are mine, and I will prove it to you moving forward. What did you come in here for?" He places a kiss on my neck and steps back.

"I came in to tell you that my grandfather is Capo Lark Caladria. He will be in town next week to see me, and he wants to set a meet-up with you." I smirk at him as I turn and leave the office, his warm cum sitting in my panties, rubbing my lips as I sway my hips down the hall.

Chapter Seven

Spyder

I STARE AT LARKIN AS she leaves my office, watching her hips sway back and forth before realizing what she just said.

"Wait, what? Who the hell did you say was wanting to meet with me!" I yell out into the hallway, not receiving any reply back. Looking through the door, I see that the hallway is already empty.

Realizing that my cock is still hanging out of my pants, I quickly tuck it back in and phone down to human resources.

My head of human resources, Mollie, answers with her ever chipper voice on the second ring.

"Human Resources, this is Mollie. Speaking, how may I help you today?"

Smiling, I remember the day she arrived at the club through the help wanted ad I had placed in the local paper.

She came into the human resource office with a folder. She slowly looked around the tiny office I had set up for the interviews and smiled before placing her resume in front of me.

Her sweet, no-nonsense voice stated. "Sir, you can look over my resume and all the others you have, but I will tell you right now that I will be starting here within the next twenty-four hours. I have been working in the human resources field for years, and I know what kind of club you will open. I have partaken in different types of BDSM that you want to have in the club, and I will be able to help you with hiring the right people for the job." She dropped the folder that she had carried onto my desk and took a seat.

As I opened it and started to look through it, I immediately realized that the file was about me and had a pretty detailed list of what I have done over the years, including some items that nobody should have known. I looked up at her. "how did you get..."

She simply raised her hand to stop me, "I am good at what I do. I wanted to be able to show you just how efficient I am. So, to prove my claim, I used the future master of this club to prove how deep I can reach and exactly what kind of information I can uncover."

I sat there with my mouth hanging open, looking over the file she had compiled, trying desperately not to smile at her blunt attitude.

I closed the file and laid it down on the desk, then picked up her resume and read it over again.

"You are going to start right now and start doing the background checks on the resume pile on my left. You will then bring them to my office, down the hallway, and up the stairs. You will knock and wait for me to answer before entering. If I don't answer, you will come back here and wait. We will go over them together and discuss who will work out and who won't."

My voice was firm before I laid her resume down on my file and looked her in the face.

"I like you, Mollie Flanagan, and I know that we will work well together, but know this, if you even try to cross Club Temptation or me, I will become the person you found out about in your research. Trust me. You do not want to see that demon." Mollie chuckled.

"Mr. Ryko Rymbersa, I will not do anything to jeopardize you or the club."

"Okay, then, Ms. Flanagan, welcome aboard and call me Spyder." She took my hand, shaking it and smiling.

"Thank you, and please call me Mollie. Ms. Flanagan was my mother, and I am nothing like that stuck-up bitch, when she was alive."

I smiled, then picked up my file and started walking out when I heard,

"Don't worry. You have the only file." I smiled even bigger and went downstairs to deal with the kitchen setup.

Shaking myself from the memory of first meeting Mollie, I smile.

"Is Larkin Pedience in your office at this moment?"

"Yes, she is. She is just finishing filling out the paperwork now." She softly states.

"You need something, don't you?" She knows me all too well.

"Yes, I need a full workup on her. I need to know everything about her, back to her being a baby. She said a name earlier that I didn't think I would never hear again."

"Oh, I love a challenge. When do you need it?" She purrs. The woman actually purred.

"Yesterday, I will be down in ten minutes to show her around the club and her room," I state.

"Okay, boss," I hang up the phone and go to the window that overlooks the club's main area.

The name that I heard escape from Larkin's luscious lips was the last name that I expected to hear, especially from her. The fact that she said that he was her grandfather.

Shaking my head in disbelief, I turn around and go to the fridge, grabbing a bottle of iced tea.

Please give it a quick shake before opening it up and taking a drink before actually saying his name aloud.

"Mr. Capo Lark Caladria. Wow, fifteen years since I have said that name, out loud." I take another drink and walk out of the office toward the human resource office.

"Hello, Mollie. How are you doing this morning?" I see Mollie look up from her computer and smile.

"Morning Spyder, It is a wonderful day, isn't it? Have two things for you. First, Ms. Pedience is finishing up her paperwork right now in the next room so that she will be with you in a couple of minutes, and two, I started on the favor you wanted. It should be ready soon."

At that moment, I see Larkin walk out of the side room and place the paperwork on Mollie's desk. She turns to me and smiles.

"Master Ryko, I have completed all of the paperwork you requested. What would you like me to do now?" I narrow my eyes and growl deeply at her.

Glancing at Mollie, who has raised her eyebrows and is now smirking at my response.

"Madame Larkin, when you are on the floor with clients or your other co-workers, you will address me as Spyder. And Mollie, don't smirk. It's undermining."

"Yes, sir, I will try to do better next time," Mollie responds, a smirk still playing on her lips.

"Let's continue with your orientation, and I will show you around the club." I lift my hand and offer for her to walk ahead of me. Trying desperately to keep my eyes ahead and not on the sway of her hips.

"Yes, Master Spyder." Larkin purrs as she walks out of the office. I start walking through the door, pausing to look at Mollie, now wearing a shit-eating grin on her face. "Mollie you are incorrigible."

"Yes, I am, and you love me anyway, 'Master' Spyder." I shake my head while smiling back at her before leaving the office.

"Where are we going first?" Larkin inquires while lightly caressing her neck from one ear down to the top of her blouse.

"We will start in the main area where the clients all gather before heading in the direction of their desired kink for the night. The kitchen and bar area are all manned by club-approved employees. Here at Club Temptation, there is a two-drink maximum. The guests all enter a foyer and must sign in before entering the main area. The foyer also provides a cloakroom. Finally, we have the specialty rooms, which are named for the kink that is represented in each room. Your room is named the Red Dungeon and will be fully stocked with all new ropes and anything you require."

I lead the way downstairs and around the club, answering Larkin's questions.

Finally, leading her to the hallway where some of the different pleasure rooms are located. We stopped at the end of the hallway, where a large red wooden medieval-style door was located. I watch Larkin walk up to the door and rub her hand down it.

The look on her face is that of part intrigued and part wonder as she uses both hands to caress the door all the way down to the handle. She looks up at me, wanting to open the door and find out what is on the other side.

I nod at her to go ahead, and she smiles like a kid in a candy shop as she turns the large iron handle in the middle of the door and shoves the door open silently to see a large circle foyer that has two large red leather chairs framing a set of stone stairs leading down to her room.

She walks in, looking at the LED flickering torches mounted on the walls casting shadows around the small room. "They are LED lights made to look like real torches. The staircase going down is lined with them as well."

Larkin smiles as she starts down the stairs before I stop her.

"Larkin, we need to talk," I turn around and close the door before turning back to her.

"Did you say that Capo Lark Caladria is your grandfather? That name is not one you just throw around expecting instant respect when people hear it." Larkin sighs and walks back up the stairs toward me.

"I'm sorry for blindsiding you with that Ryko, but he is my grandfather. He never mentioned you before until this morning when we talked over the phone. How do you know him, and do you know who he is?"

I open my tea and take another sip before answering, "remember when I said my foster mother overdosed and my foster father took off with his new boyfriend? Well, I ran away and lived on the streets for months. One night I made the mistake of trying to pickpocket Capo, and one of his men tried to beat me to death. Capo stopped them for some reason. He took me under his wings and raised me until I was old enough to join his business. Yes, I know who he is. He was a Mob Boss for two cities, and I was his second in command for years. My name is Ryko or the Spyder." I watch the color drain from her face as she takes a step back.

I reach up and cup the back of her head, then slightly pull her closer to me. "So, please answer this question. Why is Capo Caladria coming here to see me, and what kind of trouble are you in?"

Chapter Eight

Larkin

"SPYDER?" MY EYES WENT wide before closing them tightly. Ryko was the one man in the world I wished to save me. He didn't see because I was so young, but the night Rafael decided that he was done waiting for me. Ryko had just left the compound with his pregnant wife.

She used to flirt with all the men, letting them touch her in ways that only a man should touch a woman he intends on pleasure.

I can remember the first time I caught the pair having sex. Ryko had tied her up with beautiful intricate knots. The contrast of knots and the rope color he used sparked my interest in Shibari.

"That's what they called me because when I was out to get a person who screwed over the boss. My torture techniques always involved a flame or something to do with fire. My favorite was placing an aluminum bucket on someone's skin and taking a torch to it. Again, how do you know Boss

Caladria?" His hands go to his hips as he stands in the room. He has dubbed mine.

"I am the daughter of Genieve," I whisper as tears spark in my eyes. The day my mom left was one of the worst days of my life.

"Larky baby, I'm leaving and going to Dubai. I have met a man that's promised me a life that I deserve. You will be staying here with your Grandfather." She waves at me as she strolls out the door. No hug, no kiss, not even an 'I'll be back.' She left me to fend for myself. She left me to fight off my tormentor.

"See, babe, not even your mother wants to be around you. It's why I told her that you are mine." Rafael smirks before his hand goes into my hair and drags me from the room.

I spent hours in his dungeon being tortured and beaten. He stopped when Ryko came to the door and told him they had to leave.

Ryko didn't even look in to see what he was doing. He simply knocked on the door, told him they had to go, and left.

"You are little Larky?" Spyder's voice cracks.

"What I am about to tell you, I need you to sit and listen. I need you to not interrupt, and after, I need you to let me go home. This is hard, and not even my grandfather knows the whole story." I watched as he sat on the beautiful deep red leather couch. The sound the leather makes eases me a bit.

"Okay, continue." He whispers and leans back, hands behind his head, eyes trained on my face as I start to pace.

"When I turned thirteen, my mom decided she couldn't deal with my teenage antics and moved us into my Grandpa's house. I wasn't a bad child per se. I just didn't let her walk all over me. Grandpa saw it and protected me from her outbursts."

I take a deep breath and close my eyes as the memories flood back.

"What Grandpa didn't know and no one did was that my mom was sleeping with Rafael and had decided that because his appetite for sexual gratification was too much for her, I was the next best offer. She sold my virginity for three million dollars when my nightmare began. It started with little touches in areas that I should have been allowed to say no to..." My breathing becomes erratic, and I have to sit down on the floor, bringing my feet to my chest.

"I was allowed to say no. It was my right to tell him I didn't like it when he did that, but he never listened. He would tell me that he bought and paid for access to my body whenever he saw fit." I feel the tears spill down my cheeks as I explain the years of abuse I dealt with and how no one would listen when I asked for help, no when I begged for help.

"That went on for years, and the only thing that was able to stop him was when Grandpa found me half dead with Rafael's mark on my lower back. It was a tattoo. He used a heated cattle prod and seared it into my skin before using the other end to stab me in the gut. I was left for dead, and if Grandpa hadn't come home early, I wouldn't be alive." The tears roll down my face as I spin and lean forward, showing the R with a knife stuck in it.

"Rafael is still at large, despite my grandfather's ways of trying to find him. I moved here to protect myself. I moved here undetected to ensure that that evil man couldn't find me." I stand up and walk to the door. Looking over my shoulder, I see Ryko with his head in his hands, his body shaking, and I leave.

He doesn't get to be upset when he could have saved me. Is it his fault? No, he didn't know. No one knew. But I just re-lived my nightmare, and I truly don't have it in me to comfort him.

I have been soaking in the hot tub for an hour. The pain from telling my story to Ryko is still sitting heavily in my heart, but the body aches from crying have stopped.

Dinner has come and gone. I know that I need to order food and relax for the rest of the night, but I'm truly not hungry. After telling a story that you so desperately tried to forget, how can anyone eat?

Stepping out of the warm water, I wrap the towel around my body and head down to my kitchen to decide where I am ordering from.

I pull open the drawer and reach for my stack of flyers when the doorbell rings. I open the app on my phone to see who is standing on my front porch.

"Ryko, what is he doing here? Is that a kid?" I whisper as I look down at the bikini I am wearing.

I head to the door and throw it open when a tiny set of arms wrap around my waist.

"My daddy told me you were sad and that I needed to give you a hug before telling you a secret." I smile down at him before leaning over so he can whisper in my ear.

"My daddy has pizza, wings, chocolate cake, root beer, and candy. He and I made it all, and he said he hopes it helps you smile." Tears spring to my eyes as I rise to my feet and allow them to come in.

"I'm sorry, Larkin, for not knowing something was happening. I should have paid better attention. Please know that you are safe here. I will protect you with my life." He places his hand on my cheek, brushing his thumb across the apple of my face.

We spent the evening eating, watching movies, and laughing. His son was the life of our little party until he curled up into a ball on my couch and fell asleep.

We picked up all the garbage and headed toward the kitchen to finish cleaning up.

"Larkin, I want you to know that you are safe here. I will make sure of it." Spyder steps into my body, bringing both his hands to my face.

"Where have you been all my life? I have this connection to you that makes me want to submit and dominate in the same sentence. You drive my sense wild, and I don't want it to stop. Please give me a chance to prove it to you." He whispers so close to my mouth that the tiniest movement would have our lips connected.

"Protect me, please," I whisper before he lowers his lips to mine and slowly kisses me. His lips move against mine as he licks and sucks.

My phone chiming in the distance brings me out of the sensual feelings that have licked up my spine.

"I have to get that," I whisper before walking over to the counter and unlocking my screen.

Rafael: You're mine bitch. Even the Spyder won't stop me.

I read it again, not accepting what I saw. I close my eyes, not believing he found me before everything goes black.

Chapter Nine

Spyder

A FEW MINUTES EARLIER.

I hear Larkin quietly leave the room while keeping my head in my hands. I wanted to look up and try to stop her, to tell her that I was sorry for not being there to protect her, but I physically just couldn't do it.

The anger of what happened to her after I left goes beyond what I have ever felt before.

My entire body began to shake, and I wondered if this was what it felt like to have a panic attack. Did Larkin feel this way when she told me about the pain and suffering that she physically endured all those years?

For her to tell me what happened to her, then show me Rafael's signature mark on her back tells me exactly how strong she is and how much more she will have to endure with him still searching for her.

After what felt like an hour, I was able to calm down enough to finally stop shaking. Before slowly standing up, I look around the foyer for any sign that Larkin is still in the building. Hoping that she is waiting for me but knowing full well that she has already left the club.

I head back up to my office, the walk harder than I expected. All I want to do is run out and go to her, tell her what I feel for her. Apologize for everything, but I sit in my office staring off into space in the end. Trying to figure out what to do, did Larkin need time to herself to process what she had told me?

Dealing with my own PTSD and watching Tavis and Beth deal with theirs. I knew that it would take some alone time but making sure that she knew I was there to help and support her was important to recovering from an episode.

"Okay, enough of this moping around. Get off your ass and do something!" I growl aloud before sitting up, reaching to my bottom drawer, and grabbing one of several burner phones I had stored.

It looked like I had just been collecting old cell phones to the casual eye. They were burner phones. You use it once or twice. Then you destroy it.

I had to make a couple of calls, and one of them required a burner. I dial the number from memory, and a couple of seconds later, a familiar voice answers.

"I've been expecting your call, Ryko."

"Capo, it has been a while. How are you doing?" I try to keep a happy tone, all while gritting my teeth.

I hear Capo chuckle before answering. "I am doing good. I take it you didn't call to talk about the weather."

"No, I did not. I have learned a couple of things today that involve your granddaughter, Larkin. I have one question that needs to be answered. The rest can wait until you come here to visit." I pause, taking a deep breath, trying to keep my voice at a somewhat normal tone, but I end up letting the anger and venom come out, "Where the fuck is Rafael Restrepo?"

"Ah, and the shoe drops. I can honestly tell you I have no idea. I've had my people looking for him but with no results. He wronged Larkin and needs to be dealt with permanently."

"With all due respect, sir. I told you when he came on that Rafael was filled with evil and that he only had his personal interests at heart. He did not have the family's best interest."

"I should have listened to you, Ryko, and I am truly sorry for that. We have to sit down and talk, mend our relationship, for Larkin, but know this. If you find him first, you can exact whatever punishment you need to do. I give my blessing."

I breathe deeply, knowing that I have Capo's approval to take care of business.

"Thank you, Sir. I look forward to seeing you soon." Clicking the end button to finish off the call.

One call down and one more to go. I pick up the office phone and call Mollie.

Mollie answered more cheerful than normal, "Yes, Master Spyder, what can I do for you?"

"I have a new job for you. It goes along with your search into Larkin." I growl.

"Do you remember coming across a man named Rafael Restrepo during your research on me? He will come up in her past if you haven't already found it. I need you to start searching for him as well. Fair warning, Mollie, Restrepo is a bad man in worse ways than I ever could be, so I need you to be very careful during your search. I need everything you can find on both as soon as possible." I pause, taking a deep breath to let her understand the seriousness of what I just told her.

"I'll set everything aside and work on this. I'll contact Chad from Tavis's security company to help." She pauses before asking.

"Ryko, are we in danger?" I take a deep breath before answering.

"Mollie, my darling. I am not going to lie, Larkin and I will be the main targets, but there is a very good chance that others may get hurt. Be careful, please."

I end the call and call Smyth. "Yes, Boss, what do you need?"

The one thing I like about him is that he is straight and to the point. "I need you to up the security to Level Two, add guards at all doors going into the offices and the pleasure rooms. I need you to make sure that there is a mix of undercover and in plain sight. Sending you over a picture of the perp, but there is a very good chance that he will use his flunkies. And Smyth? He is very dangerous." I hear different orders being issued to his team as I continue speaking with him, but I know that he heard everything I said.

"Boss, do you need a guard? Obvious or hidden?"

"Hidden, and I need you to contact Chad at Tavis' security firm. He needs to do a full sweep of my house, the club, Larkin's place, and I may ask him to go on to the safehouse to make sure."

"Yes, sir, we will get it done."

I look at the time and see that it is noon. I decided the safest place for my son was with me. I call Tanner's school as I leave the club.

"Hi, this is Tanner Rymbersa's dad, Ryko. I am heading to pick up Tanner from school a little early. I will be leaving in a few minutes."

"Sure, Mr. Rymbersa, we can have him ready for pick up. Is this for a doctor's appointment?"

"No, for personal reasons. Please have Tanner's teachers email me any homework that needs to be done. Thank you."

Ending the call before they ask anything else. The less they know, the better.

Ten minutes later, I pull up to the school and see that Tanner and the principal are waiting for me.

I get out and open the back door for Tanner. "Hi buddy, how was school today?"

Tanner hugged me and then looked up at me. "I thought that my nanny was picking me up today?"

"Nope, change of plans, but I'll tell you in the car." He nods and climbs into the SUV.

"Thank you for bringing him out for me today. Something came up, and I need him home."

Ms. Ewing smiles politely but has a flash of concern in her eyes. "I hope that everything is okay, and if you need anything, please feel free to call me."

"I will, thank you again," I reply as I shake her hand.

She nods and turns slightly to Tanner. "Okay, Tanner, I will see you when you come back, have fun with your dad."

She waves at us, walking back toward the school, disappearing behind the heavy steel door.

I hop back into the car and place a call to the nanny. On the second ring, she picks up. "Hi, Spyder, what's up?"

"Hi, Lizzie, I just wanted to let you know that I picked Tanner up from school, so you don't have to today."

"Is everything okay? Anything I can do for you?" She asks with genuine concern.

Lizzie has been the best nanny that I've found for Tanner. She loves taking care of him and is always willing to help.

"No, we are good. I just wanted to have some time with him this afternoon before he visits his friend tonight."

"Okay then, if you need me tonight, give me a call. Say hi to Tanner for me." Tanner smiles big,

"Hi, Lizzie!" Lizzie giggles.

"Hi, Tanner, mind your dad, and I will see you tomorrow!"

"Okay, Lizzie, bye!" I chuckle as Lizzie laughs before she ends the call.

"Okay, Dad, what are we going to do?"

I turn around and look at him. "We will head home and make our special homemade pizza for my friend, Larkin. She had a bad day at work, and I think we need to cheer her up."

Tanner smiles. "Yippie! And I get to see the girl that makes you happy!"

Smiling deeply, I head back to the house, wondering how this afternoon will go.

✱ ✱ ✱

The afternoon went great. Not only did we make pizza, but he also convinced me to make chicken wings and a chocolate cake.

We showed up at her house, and Tanner rang the doorbell. "She will be surprised with us bringing dinner and dessert, Dad." He chimes as he rings the bell again.

"Buddy, she is going to be very surprised about everything." I was able to say as she opened the door, and I see her in nothing but a bikini with little unicorns all over. My heart skips a beat, and I realize what I felt earlier. I have fallen in love with Larkin, and nothing will come between us.

The rest of the night goes exactly like I hoped it would. I see Larkin's heart melt when Tanner keeps hugging her and insists on doing everything for her. We watched movies and laughed at everything he did.

Finally, after Tanner had fallen asleep on the couch, Larkin and I gathered all the garbage from the living room and headed into the kitchen.

"Larkin, I want you to know that you are safe here. I will make sure of it." I step close to her body and cup the side of her face with both hands.

Slowly moving my head closer to hers, our lips inches from touching, whispering so low that I barely hear what is said. "Where have you been all my life? I feel this connection to you makes me want to submit to you and dominate you in the same sentence. You drive my senses wild, and I don't want it to stop. Please give me a chance to prove it to you."

"Protect me, please," She whispers back, a look of love filled with desire sparkling in her eyes. I softly kiss her while slightly biting her bottom lip.

We hear her phone chime with a text notification, breaking the spell and making me moan in annoyance.

Larkin pulls away with a disappointed look on her face. "I have to get that," she walks over to the counter and picks up her phone.

I watch her look at her phone just as her face goes blank and pure terror falls across her beautiful features. Her mouth twitches, she starts to sway, and I lunge for her as she passes out.

I catch her and carefully lay her on the floor. "Larkin!" I snatch her phone off the floor and look to see what caused her to pass out. What I see makes me see red.

Rafael: You're mine bitch. Even the great Spyder won't stop me.

Picking Larkin up off the floor, I carry her to her bedroom, placing her in the middle before gently covering her body.

Heading back into the living room to ensure that Tanner is still asleep. I pick up my phone and head back to the bedroom, sitting next to Larkin. Quickly search for Smyth's number and dial.

"All good, Boss?"

"No, it's not. I need you and one other member here at Larkin Pedience's house and bring your kit that sweeps for bugs or devices that can pick up a conversation. Please, be discreet."

I hear, "yes, Boss," as I end the call and look back at Larkin's now peaceful and innocent-looking face. Taking her limp hand in mine, I whisper, "I will protect you with my life, I promise."

Chapter Ten

Larkin

"YOU LIKE WHEN I TOUCH *you there?" His gruff voice speaks into my ear, saliva from his mouth landing on my ear and neck. Making me fight my gag reflex.*

"Why do you do this?" I sob, trying to push him off of me. His body is so heavy, and his breath smells like shit mixed with alcohol. I try hard to make him roll off me, but he is glued to my body.

"Why do I do this? Because I am owed. Your mother promised that I would be hers and then ran away. So everything that I was planning on doing with her, I plan on doing that and more with you." He drags his rough hands up the inside of my thigh.

"My Grandpa will kill you," I growl, trying to close my legs, my nails digging into the skin of his chest.

He moans, "harder. I like it when women fight. It gets my dick hard." He lifted the hand on my leg and pinched my nipple, grabbing more of my breast than he should have.

"Please, stop." I sob, turning my head to the side, letting the tears fall free. I know that I won't get out of this unscathed. I know that this man will have all of me without my consent if something doesn't happen soon.

"Fight me bitch." He slaps my breast and places his hand around my neck, and slowly starts to add pressure.

I close my eyes, thinking of happier times with my Grandpa and Spyder. Went to the beach and watched as Grandpa worked and Spyder walked around making sure everything was safe.

I can feel his hand tightening more as tears run down my cheeks and as I gasp for air...

My eyes fly open as I jerk up into a sitting position. Taking in my surroundings, I notice that I am not in Grandpa's house. I am in the bed I bought, and as my eyes slowly begin to focus, my bedroom comes into view. I am safe in my home. A small hand wraps tightly in mine. I look to my left and see Tanner curled up with my sloth. The one that Grandma got me for Christmas.

Lying back down and wrapping my arm around Tanner, I take a deep breath and hold it before slowly letting it go.

Falling asleep feeling safe, at least for the time being.

* * *

"Sh Dad, you'll wake my friend Larky." Tanner's stern voice makes me smile.

"Okay, little man, I just wanted to make sure that she has some coffee and orange juice," Ryko whispers as the delectable smell of coffee hits my senses.

"I know, dad, but my girlfriend had a rough night last night." His tone makes me giggle.

"You're girlfriend, huh? I think she may be too old for you, but she is perfect for me." Ryko says, causing my insides to heat, and I know that red has flushed across my skin.

"No, Dad, you are old. She is perfect." I can't help but burst out laughing, and as I open my covers and capture Tanner, he squeals.

"Your girlfriend, huh." I start to tickle him when the covers are thrown off us, and Ryko stands there with a huge smile.

"Daddy, help, she is going to make me pee." Tanner's screams fill the room, along with his laughter.

"My sweet boy, I shouldn't come between a lovers tickle fight." Ryko steps back and raises his hand to his chin.

"Larkin, I'm going to pee!" He squeals as he gets out of my grasp and dashes for the bathroom.

I sit up in bed and look around the room, the curtains are open, and the sun is shining bright.

"So, it looks like I missed my shot again. You already have a boyfriend." Ryko whispers as he leans over me. His nose runs against my face as his lips place gentle kisses on my cheek.

"I don't know if you should be kissing me like this. My boyfriend may get mad," I whisper as I turn my head, my lips touching his as I speak.

"I think I can take him and rescue my fair maiden." He leans in and kisses me, his lips slowly caressing mine before the doorbell rings.

"Whoever that is, has the worst timing ever," I whisper and smile when he nods his head and straightens. My eyes slowly run down his body as his hand reaches for the bulge in his pants. He winks at me and turns to leave the room.

"Larkin, you going to come and have some breakfast with me?" Tanner's words clear my horny brain.

"I will meet you downstairs. Let me get dressed, and then I will meet you at the table, okay, honey?" He smiles and turns, running out of the room, slamming the door behind him.

Closing my eyes, I take a deep breath. They had to witness my fall from grace. Years of suppressing the fear that he would find me. That he would finish breaking me came to a boiling point with one simple message.

I knew I needed to contact my Grandpa, but I did not want to go back to Vegas. I don't want to go and live with my Grandfather again. His house is huge and stunning, but it's lonely.

Sighing, I stand up and head toward the bathroom. A shower is what I need to start this day.

The heat from the water caressing my skin makes my muscles relax. I close my eyes, letting go of the nightmare that had riddled my thoughts and the one that I know I am currently living.

I hear a knock on the bathroom door and smile, knowing that Tanner is just as impatient for breakfast as I am.

"Hold up, Lil man. I am just drying off, and then I will be right out." I say loudly and get no response.

Hanging up my towel on the rack and grabbing the robe off the back of the door, I swing it open and pause. Sticking my head out of the bathroom door and looking around, I notice that my window is open, and my curtains are hanging out the window.

Holding my breath, I walk toward the bed. Looking around to see if anything was out of place other than my sloth that landed on the floor during our tickle fight. Stepping to the window, I look around. Everything is quiet. Closing the window and engaging the lock, I turn and start to pick up the small mess on the floor before heading to my closet.

Searching through my clothes, I decide on a flowy summer dress and strappy sandals. I have two men downstairs that I have to impress now. Sitting down at my make-up desk, I begin to apply the moisturizer to my face.

Smelling to myself as I remember waking up snuggling with Tanner and how safe I felt knowing that Ryko wouldn't let anything happen to me. He will make sure that Rafael never gets his hands on me again.

As I am adding eyeshadow to my right eye, my phone rings on my nightstand. I knew that I needed to check in with my Grandpa, so I rushed to pick up the ringing device.

"Good morning," A smile hits my lips as I remember the last conversation I had with my grandfather.

"You were expecting someone different. Weren't you slut." His voice alone sends a shiver down my spine.

"R-R-Rafael?"

"That's right cunt. Here I am thinking that no one will want to touch some nasty ass bitch, who was used as a chew toy and thrown in the corner. But the Spyder? I figured that fucker would have sniffed my scent on your skin."

"Rafael, how...how...how did you get my number?" My breathing becomes faster. I want nothing more than to think that this man isn't anywhere close to me.

"I asked you a fucking question bitch. Did you let Spyder near my pussy?" His voice raises, and my body begins to shake

"How did you get my number?" I need to regain my control. I need to stand up to my abuser. I have people in my corner that I know will support me.

"You little bitch, you think you can get an attitude with your owner. Fuck around and find out!" I hear his laughter as the phone clicks, signaling that he has hung up.

"SON OF A BITCH!" I screamed, he is hear, this is why my window was open, he was here, in my room. He invaded my safety!

Slowly creeping toward my window, I pull the curtain back and scan the street.

"Larkin!" Ryko's voice is panicked as my door flies open, with him and my Grandpa flying to save me.

"Grandpa?" I stare at him for a little bit before launching myself into his arms.

"It's okay, my sweet princess. Are you okay?" The scent of his cigar and honey was always a soothing smell but mixed with Ryko's cologne, my heart calmed, and my mind reminded me that I was safe.

"He was in my room. He climbed through the window. How the hell did he find me?" I step back and put my hands on my hips. I forget that I am naked under the robe that is currently gapping open.

Ryko's eyes follow the opening of my housecoat before clearing his throat and asking.

I point to the bed, "I didn't see anything other than my sloth on the floor. I assumed it was from our tickle war."

"Do you use gloves to clean with?" I nod and tell him underneath the bathroom sink, watching as he goes to the bathroom and leans over to reach under the sink before turning and coming back.

"Okay, let's see if anything was left with it," Grandpa states and nods for Ryko to look around. A couple of seconds later, he finds an envelope that I missed. He brings it over and opens the letter, encouraging me to see what it says.

Larkin, Larkin, Larkin. Did you think I didn't know where you were? Your one downfall was telling someone where you were. Loyalties lie with those who have the most to gain. You need to choose your friends wiser, or maybe it's a family member.

The Spyder won't stop what's coming for you.

Someone close to me is in bed with the devil, and I have no clue who it is. How am I supposed to feel safe when my closest enemy is someone I am supposed to trust.

Chapter Eleven

Unknown

"WHAT ARE YOU DOING?" I yell at Rafael as he paces around the small hotel room. I was supposed to plant the stuff, open the window and leave the room.

"I am taking what is mine. The Spyder won't have her until her virgin blood is on my hands." He growls.

Rafael has truly lost his mind. Larkin hasn't been a virgin for some time, and knowing Ryko as good as I do, he will have already had some part of his body deep inside her.

"What did you put in the letter?" I raise my hand to my forehead and rub my temples with my thumb and pointer finger. The headache forming behind my eyes makes it hard to stay focused.

"You don't need to know that." He mumbles as he sits at the small table, pulls out his phone, and starts playing a game with the speaker on full blast.

"I did what you asked, now give me my money and release my wife." He starts to laugh before turning his head and looking at me.

"You seriously think that was all I wanted you for. You bitch of a wife is fulfilling her duties and servicing me whenever I need to get my mind off Larkin." I see red. I don't know how he got the jump on me, but watching him drag my wife away while my kids cried.

"Fuck that, you said this, and then she would be released!" I yell and watch in horror as he pulls out a gun, aims at my knee, and pulls the trigger.

"My game. My rules. When this is done, Larkin will be nothing but a broken, useless female." He looks back at his phone, mumbling something low to himself.

The burning through my knee is unbearable, but this monster can't know that I won't let him hurt anyone else.

I close my eyes, focusing on fighting through the pain. I hear him make a call and demand someone come to his room before I blackout, the pain being too much for one person to bear.

"Please, my love, fight for yourself. Fight for us, fight to survive anything that he is going to do to you." Before deciding that this man won't hurt anyone else anymore, I think to myself. I will kill him if I have to.

I just hope that in the end, I am forgiven for my actions in this fucked up plot.

Chapter Twelve

Spyder

AFTER SITTING WITH Larkin for a couple of minutes, I realized I needed to get shit done, and sitting here was not doing it.

I kiss her on the forehead before heading to the living room and getting Tanner.

Carrying him back into Larkin's room, I place him next to her with the stuffed sloth that had been sitting on the nightstand.

Looking at my watch, I realize it's almost midnight, with no sign of Smyth.

I heard a knock on the front door. Cautiously heading toward the door and looking at the doorbell screen. Sighing at the sight of Smyth standing on the other side. I open the door and look him in the eyes, "you're late."

"Sorry boss, I was finishing up at your house when you called. It is all secure, and all safety measurements are active, same with the club." He walks in, motioning to his partner to stay quiet and start the sweep.

He quickly walks through, placing his gear on the kitchen counter. I am looking at me as I motion for him to start in the back, flashing him two fingers that show two people are in the bedroom. He nods and heads back there.

Smyth hands me a thick envelope, then starts the sweep in the kitchen. I wait until he gives me the all-clear before opening the envelope. Mollie's research is neatly clipped, ready for me to look at. Everything she could find on Rafael and Larkin. Rock, would have none of it.

He contacted me twice, informing me of Rafael's status and that he was trying to gear up and take over the business from Capo. I gave him a few suggestions on what to do, but I did not have my head in the game.

By its looks, he disappeared right after he put Larkin in the hospital. He pops up here and there worldwide but vanishes just as fast.

I'm sure he was doing side deals while in the family, and he just leverages everything to full time after leaving, which means he has money and resources available.

Setting the papers down, I waited for Smyth and his second in command to finish before talking to them and making phone calls.

"All good, Boss, her apartment is clean, and he will do a scan as best as he can outside, considering where we are."

I nod as the other guard heads to the door. "Hey, keep your head on a swivel and suspect everything. This man is dangerous." He nods and walks out.

"Is my shadow here?" I ask Smyth.

"Yes, sir, he is outside in the black SUV and will be relieved in one hour." I nod and head to my jacket to pull out my burner phone. Flipping it open before pausing. "Tell him and his relief to be careful. Rafael is someone not to be underestimated. I need you to call Tavis and warn him about the situation. I don't need them to come home to a nasty surprise."

"Yes, boss, I will take care of it. If you need anything, call me." Smyth states, then walks out and closes the door.

I dial the familiar number again, hearing the click of the person answering, "Ryko, what can I do for you?" Capo asks with a hint of concern.

"He contacted Larkin tonight. I would like you to be here as soon as possible. I'm at her apartment."

"Understood. I will be there by morning. Guard her with your life, please." The click lets me know that the call has ended. I sit down on the couch and watch the door.

* * *

The next morning, I make a pot of coffee. I want to wake Larkin with the fresh scent of brewing caffeine.

Walking into the bedroom, I see Tanner cuddled up close to her. They are whispering about how she is his girlfriend. It brings a smile to my lips, knowing that we are on the same page.

"Breakfast is ready, buddy. Why don't you go to the bathroom and get cleaned up before you eat, yeah?" Tanner smiles at me and jumps from the bed.

"Good Morning, Larkin," I whisper, leaning over, taking in her sleepy smile. I lowered my face closer to hers and whispered that I was going to kiss her.

As our lips connect, my heart beats faster, and my soul eases. It's like she is breathing life into my soul. No other woman has ever faced my demons and won. I want to tell her that when the doorbell rings.

I know who it is, and after caressing her face, I get up to answer it, grabbing my defense device and sliding it up my left arm before sliding my jacket on.

"Hello Sir, please come in," I say as I open the door for Capo Caladira, stepping back and motioning for them to enter.

One guard storms in, shoving me to the wall while grabbing for his gun. I grab the back of his head, pulling him close and whispering, "be very careful with your next move, boy."

Sliding my hand around his face and pulling it in the opposite direction allows me to twist him enough to spin and slam his face into the wall. My free hand grabs the gun in his back holster and presses it to the back of his head, flipping off the safety.

The other guard rushes toward me, spinning out. I lift my other arm, activating the burner on the mini flamethrower.

Seeing a three-inch flame shooting out from my hand toward his face stops him in his tracks while still trying to pull his gun out.

"This house is under the protection of Spyder. I suggest you stand down or prepare to meet the reaper."

"Yes, boys, you need to stand down. I am safe here." Capo calmly states as he walks in. I turn off the burner while stepping back from the guard I had pinned against the wall.

He turns around and looks at me in awe, fear set in his eyes. I hand his gun back, then motion for the one to go to the living room and the other to stay by the door.

They both look at Capo, who nods before approaching me and lifting his hand, "You haven't lost your touch Ryko. But all I can see is Spyder." I reach out and grasp his hand, bowing my head slightly.

"Only when I need to be, sir. And please address me as Spyder. Very few know my true name, and I would like to keep it that way." Tanner comes running into the room smiling before seeing everyone and stops with a look of intrigue written on his little face. He slowly scans the room, taking in all the new faces before stopping on Capo. He stares for a couple of seconds before stating, "You must be Larkin's grandpappy. You look like her."

I couldn't help but chuckle as Capo smiled broadly, "Yes, I am her grandfather, little man. May I ask who you are?"

"You may," Tanner states with a flat tone while crossing his arms. Not knowing what to expect, I look at both Tanner and Capo as Capo steps forward, smiling, and extends his hand.

"Hello little master, my name is Capo Lark Caladria. And your name is?" Tanner smiles and takes his hand firmly in his little one and shakes it.

"My name is Tanner Ryko Rymbersa. Nice to meet you. Are you here for breakfast?"

"I would enjoy that. Are you fixing breakfast this morning?" Capo laughs lightly at Tanner's answer, "only if you like cereal and fruit."

"Sounds great, I would…" was all Capo could get out before "SON OF A BITCH!" Rattles through the house. Capo and I look at each other before I point to the guard at the door.

"You, outside, circle the apartment now! Tanner, stay here with the gentlemen in the living room." Capo nods then we take off at a dead run to the bedroom as I pull out my gun, not knowing what to expect but knowing that my fears will turn into reality.

Chapter Thirteen

Larkin

I CAN'T BELIEVE THAT someone close to me is in bed with the man that spent years torturing me. Rafael is a piece of shit, and he spent my teenage years making sure that he used and abused me every way he knew how.

My fucking family let him. My mother walked away, leaving me to fend off the demon himself.

My phone vibrates on the table. I have never been so pissed off at a device as I am right now. I'd like to grab my phone and shove it down his throat.

"What the fuck do you want?"

"Spyder, you let Spyder fuck that pretty little cunt of yours?"

"Rafael, how about this. You go find a hooker and leave me the fuck alone. You've done enough fucking damage to me physically and mentally."

"I asked you a fucking question bitch. Did you let Spyder near my pussy?"

"And I told you to fuck off."

"You little bitch, you think you can get an attitude with your owner. Fuck around and find out! Simply for my fucking pleasure, go to the window, and look down." He chuckles before he hangs up.

Jumping out of my bed, I run to the window and see Rafael standing at the end of my driveway, holding my dog by the scruff of the neck. I step closer to the window and notice that he has a mass stuck to the side of my car.

"SON OF A BITCH!" I scream as my car explodes, and I watch in horror as Rafael throws my dog.

The explosion rocked my townhouse, tossing car pieces against the building. I watch from my window in horror as he simply walks away waving. Just before he disappears, he stops and points with his finger to where he can see me and then runs his finger across his neck.

Placing my hand on the window, I let the frustration take over. I want nothing more than to stand over his body as I drain the life out of him.

My door comes flying open as Ryko and my grandfather comes flying in. Ryko has his gun raised, and my grandfather looks like he signed a million dollars away to a fake account.

"You hurt?" was all my grandfather got out as I hugged him. I told them what happened on the phone and the explosion outside. After finding and reading what the letter said, we stood there wondering what to do next when the door busted open, causing Ryko to whip his gun out.

"What the fuck?" Ryko growls as Tanner runs into the room, passing by his dad and my grandfather and crashing into my body.

"My Larky, are you okay?" He cries as his little arms hug my waist tighter.

"Hey, buddy, look at me, yeah?" He raises his head and looks at me, "I am okay, sweetheart, I promise. Wipe your tears, and let's show the men behind you how strong you are, yeah?"

He stands straight and turns toward his dad. "I'm disappointed in you, Dad." His little arms fold across his chest, forcing Spyder to put his gun away.

"Why are you disappointed in me?" Spyder asks with a small smirk playing on his handsome face.

"You didn't make sure my Larky was okay when you came into the room. You said a bad word and just stood there. I will have to talk to Uncle Tavis to see if he can help me protect her cause you can't." He stomps out of the room.

My grandfather chuckles before coming to me and wrapping me in a hug. "Get dressed and then come downstairs and tell me what happened. I need to smooth things out with your boyfriend down there." He chuckles and walks to Tanner, shakes his head, and leaves the room, closing the door behind him.

"I think I will have to duel my son for your hand." He shakes his head and chuckles.

"Rafael was outside. That explosion was him blowing up my car. He knows that we are sleeping together." I rattle off what I remember.

"Larkin, come here, yeah?" He whispers.

I take the first step before launching myself into his body, wrapping my legs around his waist.

"Ryko, I'm scared," I whisper into his neck. His hands go to my ass.

"I promise you this, Larkin, I will set the world on fire before that asshole ever touches a single hair on your body. Tell me what happened?"

Raising my head, I look into his eyes and slam my lips onto his before quickly pulling away, "let me put some clothes on, and then we can go downstairs. I can fill you and grandpa in on what happened. I have a feeling Spyder that he has corrupted one of your staff members because he called my cell phone."

He stares at me, "Your number is public, is it not?"

I shake my head, "No, my number is unlisted and under a fake name and address. No one knows that it's my number but you and your staff."

I walk toward my bathroom and close the door.

"So, what you're telling me, is that Ryko has someone double-crossing him, and the only way to find out is to flush them out?" My grandfather questions.

"Yes, if I can get them to admit that they gave my number out, we can find out where Rafael is." I shrug.

"Not happening, we will find out who it was another way, but I will not use you as bait." Spyder roars.

"Okay, there, caveman! Did you even listen to my reasoning?" I growl at him. We stand there and stare at each other.

"Hey, Tanner, why don't you and I go out to dinner. Let's let your dad and my granddaughter have a boring adult discussion while we go out and have fun." My grandfather says, leaving the room.

Spyder and I stare at each other as we hear the front door slam.

"You are not doing it, and that's the end of this discussion," Spyder growls while taking a step closer to me.

"It's the only way, Ryko, and you know it. If it's not me asking questions, no one will tell you anything." He steps closer to me as his hands go into my hair.

"I won't lose you when I just found you. I will go to the ends of the earth to make sure that I still have you in my life and Tanner's. Please let's come up with another solution. I promise to agree to anything, just not putting yourself in danger." His lips crash to mine as he slowly shows me how much he needs me.

This is primal possession. He wants me forever, not just a fly-by-the-night fuck fest.

"Ryko, I promise I will..." I am cut off by scratching at the door. Spyder raises his finger to his lips and makes his way quietly to open the door. My dog walks in like he has been out with the neighbor's female dog all night.

As Spyder closes the door, a shot splinters the door and causes him to fall to the ground unconscious.

Chapter Fourteen

Spyder

THE EXPLOSION RADDLES the windows of the townhouse as we hear Larkin scream, both Capo and I recognize the sound of a car explosion immediately and know we are on a time limit

We ran upstairs to check on Larkin and find out what had happened. Was Rafael behind it? The thought had my blood start boiling. He just placed a big target on everyone I loved.

Coming back downstairs, I see Capo and Tanner sitting in the kitchen eating a banana with the bodyguard pacing everywhere. I walk up to the table and sit down.

"We have a problem, Sir, I need to make sure that you and Larkin are safe, but I don't have the time to hide you. I take it that you have a couple of fake IDs like usual?"

"Of course I do, Get my briefcase from the car and check to ensure that everyone is on high alert. He should be still circling the apartment." His main guard nods looks toward me then leaves the apartment, closing the door quietly.

Turning to Tanner, I look into his eyes to see how he is, not a hint of fear emanating from his baby blue eyes. Kid takes after me more than I ever thought.

"Lil Man, do you have any questions about what happened? That must have been pretty scary for you." I ask while watching his every movement.

He takes a bite of his banana and then answers after swallowing. "No, Daddy, Grandpappy explained that a bad guy is trying to hurt my Larky, and you will stop him."

"Yes, I am. This bad man has been a bane in my life since he came into it when I worked for," pausing to look at Capo, who was smiling at my upcoming response.

"Grandpappy years ago. He tried to hurt both of them before, and I will not let that happen again." Hearing the door starting to open, I pulled my gun and aimed for the center of the door as the two guards entered.

They close the door and stand guard while the other brings the briefcase to the table and lays it down, turning it to face Capo before heading upstairs to stand guard.

I put my gun away and faced Capo as we started hearing the sirens in the distance.

"Okay, time is up. We need to get our secret identities ready we both know that the police will be asking for them as soon as they roll-up. You are Laurence, and you are here to visit your granddaughter Larkin. Tanner, you stay with Grandpappy and do not leave his side unless you are with Larkin." I stand up and call for the guard upstairs. "You two need to be his servants, and for the love of everything, try not to look like you just came out of a mobster movie. I will see what I can do with the circus about to show up." Just like that, I am back in the family business, one I fought tooth and nail to get out of years ago.

* * *

WATCHING THE AREA AS the lights bounce off the windows, the fire and police rolled up to the scene. I look to Larkin, who I have wrapped up in a blanket, and start to construct a story. With everyone that is around me, we piece together a story.

As the first of the officers show up, I see a familiar face in the crowd, "Officer Chepte, it's been a while." I called out as I moved Larkin to stand in front of me.

Chepte walks up and shakes my hand. "It's been a while, Spyder. I would say it was a good morning," pausing to wave his hand at the burning car that the fire department is working to put out.

"But this will ruin anyone's day." Chepte looks back at me, then turns serious. "We have a history, so I will be blunt and off the record. Does this have anything to do with Tavis?"

"Off the record, no, but it does have to do with my past. There are a couple of people inside of the townhouse that have deep ties to the Caladira mafia."

Chepte narrows his eyes and then asks in a hushed tone. "Who is in the house that I need to worry about. Will it affect the safety of this city?"

"Off the record, it's Boss Capo Caladria, but he is going by Laurence. He is under my protection, and I prefer if you don't have to talk to him. Can you make it look like the explosion was a gas leak set off by the car alarm or something like that? The car belongs to Miss. Pedience." I nod my head down to the woman shivering in my arms. "This was her townhouse, and Laurence is her grandfather."

Chepte closes his eyes, takes a deep breath, and looks over his shoulder to another officer. "Thomas, the gentleman here said that the owner armed the car after getting something out of it. She happened to smell gas before but didn't think of anything of it as she set the alarm on the car. Go inform the Fire Chief about what happened while I take their statements."

"Yes, Detective Chepte, do you need anything else?"

"No, I have everything I need for the statements. Just make sure that the crowds don't get in the way. Have the forensics officer in charge come see me when he gets here so I can explain what happened to him." The officer nods then rushes over to tell the fire chief exactly what he told him.

I look at Chepte with a smile. "You got promoted to Detective. Congratulations. When did that happen?"

"Couple of years ago, now let's get everyone's stories straight, so none of this bites us in the ass. I don't want anyone in jail. I do have to tell you that once the fire marshall investigates, I will get my ass fired for making shit up. Figure out a fucking way that my ass doesn't get fired, Rymbersa!"

*** * ***

A few hours later, the fire is out, and the burnt shell of Larkin's car is loaded on a flatbed and taken back to the police department. The forensics officer in charge understands what is happening and agrees to the cover-up, as long as it doesn't cause any issues. Chepte finally got the statements finished and made sure that everything matched.

We make plans in case some issues arise, but the way he did all of the paperwork, it doesn't seem to be needed. Having a plan is always good.

With the Detective finally finished and Larkin is resting in my arms, the guys are beginning to discuss the possibility of a rat close to me. The thought that whoever is close to me is selling secrets to my enemy pisses me off.

"Do you think that Rafael has paid people off for information? Think about it: if you find the right person who is in desperate need of money, the right amount will make the take on anything. Even if it means going against your loyalties."

What gets me is that she is right and that Rafael may have gotten to others. At this point, anyone that is close to me could have the potential to harm the ones I love.

"I won't lose you, not when I just found you. I will go to the ends of the earth to make sure that I still have you in mine and Tanner's lives. Please let's come up with another solution. I promise to agree to anything, just not putting yourself in danger." I state in a hushed tone before kissing her.

Knowing that I love her and want her to be mine forever makes my determination to end this madness quickly a priority. No one else will get hurt on my watch, including my woman.

Larkin pulls away, finally looking up at me, questions written all over her face, and I know that she wants to know how I will be able to keep her safe.

"Ryko, I promise like that..." is all she gets out when we hear scratching at the door.

The guards have left with Capo and Tanner earlier, so I know that we are alone.

I motioned for her to keep quiet as I slowly walked to the side of the door and looked at the door cam. What I see on the screen in front of me surprises me.

I see her dog sitting at the door, his fur is a little black, and he has a slight limp. But we thought he was dead, I open the door for him to walk in, and he struts in like he owns the place.

I close the door and turn toward Larkin when I feel a sharp sting hit me in the back. As I hit the ground, my last thought is that I keep letting my guard down around this woman, and I think it may have just bit me in the ass. The old Spyder will need to come forward and show everyone how ruthless I can be.

Larkin's screams could wake the dead. The way she is carrying on, you would think something major happened.

"Damn it stop fucking screaming! I hear you!" I mumble as I start to sit up, reaching for the gun sitting inside my jacket.

"You got shot! Don't move!" Larkin sobs, tears running down her face.

"I'm okay, babe. I came prepared for something like this." I pull back my shirt and show her my bulletproof vest, resting over my chest and under my shirt. She gasps and then hugs me tightly.

"Easy woman, that round still hurt like hell. I'm going to have a bruise the size of someone's foot on my chest. It could have been a lot worse."

I pull out my burner phone and call Capo.

"The house has been compromised. Stay away. I will contact you with directions to a safe house when the time is right. Tell Tanner that Larkin and I both love him." I hang up and then slowly stand with Larkin's assistance.

"Safehouse?" is all she gets out as my shadow runs into the house.

"Boss you, okay?"

"Yeah, no thanks to you! Now go try to find the fucker that shot me!" I growl, dialing the last number that I ever expected to use and hadn't since I left the family all those years ago.

"Spyder, it's been a while." The voice states after the first ring.

"Chrome, how fast can you get my team back together."

"Sir, we never disbanded. We worked for Boss after you left the family. Our loyalty will always be to you and your loved ones. We are here at your command."

"Swear your allegiance to me. Swear that you will sacrifice your life to protect my loved ones. Swear that you will stand by my side and help me bring peace back to our family." I heard the phone click to the speaker then a booming round of deep voices echoed.

"We swear, Spyder, we stand by you to fight with you. We stand in front of you to protect you, and we will never stand behind you unless we are watching your back."

I smile at Larkin's confused look as her face becomes even more puzzled.

"I am in the wind. I need you here, and I need the safe house secured. My current safe house is compromised. Capo is here with me and will be at the safe house along with Larkin. I need you to get Mrs. Caladria to the same place we will be heading, and I needed her there yesterday. We are under attack."

"Spyder, we know that Capo is with you. I have already made arrangements, and we are in the area. We will be there in five minutes. We know the address. The car bomb set the media a flurry, which told us where to find you." The call ends.

Looking down at my arm, I see that the vest didn't fully protect me, and I am bleeding. I start to get light-headed from the blood loss. I lie down on the floor, feeling the blackness taking over.

True to Chrome's word, they arrive within five minutes. They tell Larkin to go and get dressed, and then they pick me up and take me to the black SUV, making sure that I am covered, before turning and running back inside to get my woman.

After we get in, I turn to Chrome. "Rafael Restrepo is behind this. Knowing his mind, I can guarantee that he will have a tail on us. Make sure you are not being followed and get us to the safe house. Make sure the medic is already there as the fucker shot me or had someone else do it."

I look at Larkin, who at this point is just accepting that what is happening as part of her life.

"Babe, we are safe here with them." The pain steals my breath for the last time as I pass out, letting the blackness take me dark.

I wake up to Chrome removing me from the back SUV and into the back another. We drive down into a parking garage, twisting around the levels as we get deeper into the steel and concrete structure.

Once we park, we are ushered into a safety elevator, where level two is pressed, and the machine starts to move. I know this is where the enemy will get confused because we are technically only going up a level and a half then the back of the elevator opens up to a secret apartment.

We passed through several metal bunker doors before it opened up into a large room with maps of the city, computers with different programs, and rooms to make sure that everyone stayed safe.

They all stand at attention and slammed their fist into their chest as we entered. "Back to work."

"Okay, Sir, lie down, and I will have the medic come to you. I will show Larkin where you are as soon as she is finished talking to Capo. Spyder, if you need anything, just ask the guard standing at the door." Chrome leaves as I slowly take off my clothes before lying down on the bed.

The medic enters and finds that the wound is from a large piece of wooden shrapnel. It must have been from when the round went through the door.

"You will live to fight another day, Spyder. I would say take it easy, but I know who you are, and that won't happen."

"Thanks, Doc, you are the best," I state while adjusting the sling that he had my left arm in. He nods and then leaves the bedroom.

I know Larkin is going to be in, in a few minutes, so I strip down to my boxer briefs and lie in the middle of the bed.

I want to surprise her and assure her that I am still very much alive.

The simple thought of her calms my soul but sets fire to my body. I have never felt this with Cadace.

In this instant, my mind, body, and soul all come in sync with what I want for the rest of my life.

Chapter Fifteen

Larkin

LIFE HAS A WAY OF THROWING curveballs at you that you are never ready for. My first curveball was when my Mom gave me to Rafael, and I have just experienced my second one as I watch Ryko lying on the floor.

Everything moved in slow motion as men started to file in out of nowhere. But my focus was on the man lying on the floor. He looked so peaceful. If it weren't for his chest's shallow rise and fall, you would have thought that the blast had killed him.

"Miss? Can you stand up?" A man asks.

I have no idea who these men are, but they just referred to Ryko as Spyder. Like he is some sort of supernatural being.

"Larkin, can you stand?" The man yells like I am hard of hearing.

"I am right here, dude. You yell at me one more time, and I will have your nuts in a vice." I grumble and stand up, walking toward the sink to wash my hands.

"We have to move you and Spyder to the safe house. Can you go upstairs and pack a light bag?" I look at the man standing to my right. He has been with my Grandpa for years, but he normally watches the outside wall.

As I turn to dry my hands, he sighs, "Larkin, please can you go and pack a bag?"

I nod and walk past him as men quickly work to stop Ryko from bleeding. My life has always been filled with men everywhere. For one moment in time, I had quiet. I had solitude.

Falling in love with Ryko will take that away, but I am okay with that. I am okay with never having a quiet place. I am ok with constantly being surrounded by men whose sole purpose is to protect my family and me.

I need to make sure that Ryko is on the same page because I can't see my future without Ryko and Tanner sharing the stage with me.

***

The move to the safe house was made in the dead of night. So, when we finally arrived, it was no shock that my Grandmother was waiting in the kitchen with a full spread of food and a full pot of coffee.

When she looked over her shoulder and saw me, she dropped what she was doing and ran over to me, engulfing me in her arms.

"My precious girl, I am so glad you are safe." I hug her tighter and close my eyes. She may be my grandmother, but she has been the only solid motherly figure in my life for a long time.

The men carry Ryko in and turn to the left, taking him to the biggest room on the left side of the house. Grandpa comes in behind them, carrying a sleeping Tanner and turning to the right.

"You hungry precious?" Grandma asks.

"I am exhausted, grandma. I would like to go to bed and sleep for a week." She smiles and points to the left.

"You and Ryko have the left side. Your grandfather, Tanner, and I have the right. Go to sleep, my girl. We will talk when you get up in the morning." She spins me around and sends me on my way.

When I reach the end of the hall and slowly open the door to the room I am staying in with Ryko. I'm shocked. The room is huge. To one side is a king-sized bed placed in an alcove that I am one hundred percent opens up onto a balcony. The only thing separating the bed from the elements is the French doors.

To the left is a sitting area and past that is a huge bathroom. Ryko is currently sitting in the middle of the king-sized bed with his arm in a sling and a smirk on his face.

"Larkin, come here." His voice is gruff.

I walk toward the edge of the bed, slowly spinning around, swaying my hips back and forth. My hands slide down the sides of my body before I bend at the waist, making sure to pop out my ass, before sliding my hands up the inside of my legs.

"Fuck, strip for me, Larkin, nice and fucking slow." He growls.

Closing my eyes, I grind my hips as my hand slides around to unzip my pants, slowly sliding them down over my hips, revealing the peach lace panties that hug my cheeks. My pussy pulses to the sway of my hips, causing me to run my hand between my legs, rubbing the lace materials hard into my swollen clit.

"Touch yourself again, and you better be squatting over my face," Ryko growls.

"That can be arranged." I purr as I continue taking off every piece of clothing I have on. I am so on edge that as I peel the lace panties down my leg, the wetness from my slick pussy makes the material stick and pull, causing me to moan.

"Fuck, Larkin." His growls.

Spinning around, I watch Ryko throw the blanket off himself, revealing a very naked and erect man.

"It's like Christmas, Easter, and my birthday wrapped up in a silk sheet." I purr as I place my knees on the edge of the bed and slowly begin to crawl toward him.

"Fuck, I have never seen a sexier site." Ryko spreads his legs to allow me to crawl up between them.

Slowly kissing each leg as I crawl toward the trophy, standing erect and proud.

"Ryko, I want to take you in my mouth," I tell him as I run my tongue leisurely around his balls, then slowly slide up his shaft.

"Fuck, Larkin, please." He groans just as I drop a ball of spit on the tip of his dick and slide him deep into my mouth.

Ryko flexes his hips, pushing deeper into my mouth. His good hand grips my hair and pushes my head down. His being so deep in my throat causes me to gag and choke before pulling my head back and looking into Ryko's eyes.

"The sexiest thing I have ever seen is you stripping before crawling between my legs." His eyes drop to my hand as it slowly slides up and down his shaft.

"Something you like?" I purr, squeezing gently, causing Ryko to flex his hips.

"Please, please continue to crawl up my body. I want you to straddle my lap and ride me."

Crawling up his body, I straddle his lap and slide slowly down his erection. Once I have him deep inside my body, I spread my legs so he can watch as I slide my finger over my clit and bring myself to an explosive orgasm.

Ryko moans and begins to beg for me to move. A small smile plays at my mouth as I raise my fingers to his lips and demand, "clean them first."

Chapter Sixteen

Spyder

NOT ONE TO TURN DOWN an invitation like that, I grasped her hand then slowly started sucking and licking one finger, starting with her tip and then working down her finger.

I thrust my hard cock up into her as I suck hard on her finger. Larkin moans as she throws her head back and starts grinding.

Letting go of one finger and starting on the other. I feel her claws dig into my chest with her free hand as her moans slowly become louder as she starts to dry hump me.

Feeling myself getting ready to explode. I let go of her hand and reach her throat, lightly squeezing as I growl. "I am going to explode in you, cum with me, baby."

Larken nods her head as she digs both hands into my chest. As she lets out a muffled squeal, her nails dig deeper into my chest, drawing blood.

The pain from her scratches on my chest and the feeling of her pussy squeezing my shaft set my orgasm chasing hers.

She collapsed on top of me, breathing hard and fast, the smell of her sweat and sex along with mine as I wrapped my good arm around her and pulled her tight to me.

Listening to her as she falls asleep with a slight smile on her face. I kiss her on the forehead and whisper good night as I close my eyes and let her breathing lull me to sleep.

A few minutes later, I was woken up by pounding on the door. Groaning deeply, I roll over toward the door, "Whoever is knocking on that door better be ready to meet their God!"

"Sorry to disturb you, Spyder, but I was informed by Capo to awaken you and have you come into the war room."

Looking at the clock, I realized that we had been asleep for six hours.

As I slowly sit up, looking over at Larkin, who is still sound asleep and looks at peace for the first time in a while. I knew that it wouldn't last long until I could make sure Rafael was no longer a threat to anyone.

A much quieter knock echoed from the door. "What should I tell him?"

Wiping my face with my good hand, I finally answered, "Tell him I will be there as soon as possible."

"Yes, sir," He replies. Then the sound of boots rushing away catches my attention.

I slowly walk over to the bathroom, washing my face and trying to pull a comb through my hair.

Looking in the closet, I see a couple of sets of fatigues and a couple of suits. I opt for the battle look. I dressed in the black fatigues, then went to Larkin and kissed her forehead.

She moans, then rolls over, exposing her perfect breasts, not risking a hard-on before seeing everyone. I cover her up and head out the door, the guard tightening his stance as I pass by.

"If she wakes up before I get back, escort her to where I am."

"Yes, Spyder!" He snaps his reply and then goes back to guard. I quickly stride into the war room and look around.

I immediately see Capo along with Chrome and Rock at the main table, looking at some papers and a couple of monitors. I stop at the coffee table and fill a cup with the strongest coffee, walking up behind them.

"You called for me?" I inquired as I took a swig of the molten lava in my cup.

"Hope you slept well last night, Spyder, because we may have just caught a break!" Holding up a paper, he hands it to me.

I quietly scan over the contents, then look up with an inquiring look.

"Are you sure this is right, Boss? Having some of his guys show up not only at Larkin's house but also at mine, they may happen to see them, which is good and well, but this may also be a trap. Who do you have out in the field on this Chrome?"

"Five of our best, one at each house and the Club, with the other two rotating around. They check in every ten minutes with authentication codes and have to double verify every time they make contact."

"Good, we don't need any more surprises at this point. Also, one more thing, Rafael is not stupid, so that he may go after Cadace and her family. Have someone check on them to make sure that they are okay."

Capo looked at me with a puzzled look, "Your ex-wife? I thought that you two were not speaking to each other?"

I smile at the thought that he knows about my history even though we haven't spoken in years. I never hid after opening the club, but now that seems to have been a mistake.

"We had problems at the end of our marriage and after we divorced. But she took steps to become a better person, now we are good friends, and she is a great mom to Tanner. Her whole family loves Tanner and me, we have become one little unit, but it was never meant to be for her and me."

"Who doesn't love Tanner, your son is an awesome kid!" A beautiful voice from behind me speaks, sounding like my angel. I turn around and see Larkin walking up to me and putting her arms around my neck.

"I know that his dad is pretty awesome too." She whispers into my ear.

I wrap it around her waist and pull her close using my good arm. "I think you are pretty awesome yourself, babe."

Lowering my head to hers, kissing her, when we hear a very familiar voice.

"Eww! Daddy, why are you kissing my Larky? You can't do that!" Tanner runs up to us, grabbing Larkin's leg and giving it a bear hug.

Everyone in the room chuckled before Rock coughed and chimed in, "Sorry to interrupt, but I will send two men to check on your ex-wife and her family."

Turning to him, I nod. He pulls out a radio and gives a couple of commands as he walks away.

Larkin pulls back a little, "Okay, you have to explain this whole thing to me. It's freaking weird. Why do they call you that and my grandfather just Boss?"

"I do have to explain a few things to you. Let's go into the kitchen and grab something to eat. Then I will do my best to clarify all of this," I state, pulling away and cupping her face with my hand as Tanner grabs hers.

Capo smiles as he leads the way to the kitchen, where Mrs. Caladria has already set the table for us. I looked at the food on the plate, all of the extra on the counter, then glanced at Larkin, "Your Grandmother has always made a 'to die for' buffet of food. I missed her cooking."

"I can tell that you haven't been eating as you should be, Son. You are all skin and bones. Now all of you sit down and eat. There is plenty," she orders as she points to the table.

We all mutter, "Yes, Ma'am," as Tanner giggles and sits next to Larkin. As a tradition, we said grace and then started eating. After a couple of bites, I start to tell my story.

"Larkin, I grew up in the family. I had started to see that your grandfather, who was always a great man, had started to become more ruthless than he needed to be. I was already in the family by then and had just become his second in command when he started to look into doing new lines of business. I told him the businesses were not good for the family and that it would cause issues later on."

"What kind of new business?" Larkin asks.

"Don't think bad of me, but at the time, I was considering adding human trafficking to the prostitution business that we had going. There was money to be made, and at the time, that is all I cared about." Capo answers for me.

Larkin's jaw opens and closes as she stares at him, her fork halfway to her mouth, her eyes as wide as saucers.

"We talked, well, more like argued. In the end, he saw that it was a bad business deal. Not only because it involved the suffering of humans but also because we would have to deal with some very ruthless people. At that time, I needed to come up with a security backup in case your grandfather decided to become more ruthless, turning into the people we were trying to avoid. So, I started my army. Over time, I recruited and brought people in with various talents to help protect everyone and remove whatever threat that may spring up within the family. These men would do anything to protect the family, but, in the end, their absolute loyalty is and was to me. That was tested a couple of years later when Boss tried to take over a smaller area with brute force. Your grandfather was power-hungry and did not care who would get hurt. He tried to order my men and me to kill the entire family controlling the area. When we refused, he had his guards attack us, which ended in a blood bath. Your grandfather thought we were going to kill him, and I would take over. The thing is, I didn't want the power. I respect him and will die for him, but I won't let him hurt or kill people just to gain power, not that way." I grab Larkin's hand. I knew this would all be overwhelming to her, but I needed her to hear it. I need her to hear every single word that is being said.

"Spyder did me a huge service that day," Capo states with admiration in his voice.

"I vowed to become a better person and Boss in the areas I controlled. Yes, we all can be ruthless, and we have taken out the garbage many times, but in the end, the family became better for it. So, his army guards us and protects us, but I have to discuss my major plans with either Spyder or Rock to get their support. It's a check and balance system that has worked for years. The only time that I never got their full support was with Rafael. He was and still is a psycho that hid his mental illness very well." Capo looks at Larkin with a sadness that runs deep,

"He hurt you in ways that I don't know, and for that, I am sorry." I watch as Larkin gets up and hugs her grandfather long and hard, finally when she pulls away and wipes tears from her eyes. She sits back down, reaches for Tanner hugs him. Smiling at that simple reaction and how even my son can calm her down ease my heart.

Tanner whispers something into Larkin's ear, and she hands him something, then looks back at me,

"So that's why they call you Spyder and me Larkin. Wow, that is a lot to process at one time, but it all makes sense." I take her hand and squeeze it before she starts eating again. Talking with Capo and Chrome about following Rafael's men or just taking them and interrogating them.

When I hear a beep, I look around, figuring out where the noise is coming from. When I hear it again, "what is that noise?"

"Don't worry", Larkin said between bites of food, "that is my phone. Tanner is playing a game on it." I continue eating for a minute when I realize what she said.

"You have your phone with you? How long has it been on!" I snap as Chrome starts barking orders into his radio.

"What's the big deal? I turned it on when he asked to play a game on it. It's just a harmless game anyway." She shrugs.

I look her straight in the eyes and growl, "He knows your phone number, which means he can track it to us when the power is turned on. Dammit, woman, you compromised our safe house!"

Chrome comes back to the table, "I can't blind verify the guards downstairs. We may be under attack!"

The main doors explode as smoke grenades are hurled into the main room, along with a large disk that looks like a flashbang.

I grab Larkin and Tanner, shoving them toward Capo using my body as a shield for when the flash-bang goes off.

It seems to take forever for the flash-bang to go off, then suddenly a bright light blinds me, and a loud bang disorients me. Trying to regain my focus and search for my family is proving difficult. Gunfire erupts from different directions as screams fill the house. I hazily see Larkin, Capo, and Tanner being led away by Chrome when I get hit in the head from behind, knocking me to my knees. A couple of seconds later, I get kicked in the back, knocking me down to the floor.

As the sharp burning pain sears through my body, the realization sets in that at least one rib has been cracked. The kicks stopped as I rolled onto my back and looked into the face of Rafael Restrepo.

"Hello Spyder, long time no see. I see that you have been treating my property well, but as you can see, I am here to collect her." With that, he kicks me in the ribs.

"Hello Repo, or is it asswipe? I never could remember which." I cough and gasp for air. He stops smiling and then kicks me in the head. The world spins as the pain shoots through my head.

"Spyder, you can make fun all you want, but in the end, I will take Larkin back, and I will use and abuse her to my heart's content."

"She is not your property fuckface, and when I get up, I will make sure that you never bother her again." I spit out bright splatters of blood directed toward his feet. Rafael just shook his head, then pulled out his gun, pointing it at my head.

"Sorry, Spyder, neither of those options will work for me. Goodbye, Ryko," then he pulls the trigger.

Chapter Seventeen

Larkin

"NO!" I SCREAM AS I watch Repo's trigger finger start to tighten on the piece of equipment that will determine whether Ryko lives or dies.

Repo's head turns to me as he continues to press the trigger.

"You know what has to happen, Larkin. You either agree to come with me or watch as I blow his brains all over the floor."

My grandfather grabs my arm. Fear etched across his face before he shook his head.

"Larky?" Tanner's scared voice breaks my heart, and I know what I need to do.

Kneeling in front of Tanner and taking him into my arms before reaching up and grabbing my grandfather's hand. "I need to do this to ensure that Ryko is alive for Tanner. It's my fault they found us, so I need to do this. Promise me that you will always keep looking for me?"

My grandfather opens his mouth, ready to tell me, no, but I shake my head.

"Please, I need to make sure that the world still has that man in it. I will always fight, but I need your reassurance that you will never stop looking for me."

"I promise to move heaven and earth to make sure you are back in my arms. Remember what I taught you?" He asks, and I remember letting him know with a nod of my head.

I lean in and whisper in Tanner's ear, "remind them that they had a microchip implanted in my foot when they need it. I love you, Tanner."

"What's it going to be bitch? My finger is getting itchy, and I feel like redecorating the room in the color blood." Repo growls.

"I'll come with you," I say, growling as I stand and slowly make my way toward the vilest man I have ever met.

As soon as I am within reaching distance, he lashes out and grabs my arm, pulling me into his body.

"Can't wait to taste that pussy. You know I will be a better fuck than that useless piece of shit on the floor." He spins me around.

"Look at your grandfather and Spyder's brat." He growls in my ear, and I look up into the eyes of my grandfather, tears rolling down his cheek

Repo doesn't say a word as his hand runs down my throat, leaving a line of blood from the tip of my chin to the opening of my shirt. He adds a little more pressure as my shirt begins to tear away from my body. His hand grips my breast, which causes me to winch as a sharp pain shoots through my breast.

My eyes slide close, fighting back the tears that are threatening to spill down my cheeks.

The best place to drop a man is to hit between his legs with all your strength. I remember the first lesson my grandfather taught me. I know that as soon as I get the chance, I will kill Repo.

He starts to laugh as a sharp prick hits my skin, and I am thrown over the shoulder of Rock.

The last thing I see before my world goes black is Tanner's face full of sheer terror.

To Be Continued...

Join us for the epic conclusion in Cuffed to Him

About the authors

JA Lafrance

JA resides in Northern Ontario, Canada but is originally from Toronto, the capital of Ontario. She and her loving husband have three beautiful children. When she is not locked in her writing cave, she works with the board of education as a supply Educational Assistant.

She loves watching hockey and soccer and enjoys talking to the many people she has made friends with through her craft.

JA enjoys a good joke and sharing them. It is why she is seen more with a smile on her face than a frown.

Michael Mann

Michael Mann was born in southern New Mexico but has lived in several states, including Alaska. While growing up, his family traveled and visited different states, which he continued by touring Germany when serving in the Army. Michael and his family currently reside in southwest Arizona. When not writing and working, he enjoys the great outdoors, travel, cooking, photography, and spending time with family and friends.

Back Lists

JA Lafrance

Curvy and Wanted

The ECE & Her Billionaire

The Brother & Her Best Friend

The Girl & Her Men

Bleeding Miners MC

From The Darkness

What If Princess? Short Story Series

Gaston's Confession

Celebration Series: Short Stories

Daddy Santa

Daddy Hop

Others

Erotic Bedtime Story

Stunned

Her Stern Rancher

Unhinged Thoughts

A Curvy Kind of Love: Short Stories

Magic in Massachusetts

As My Heart Speaks

Tamah (Coming soon)

Co-Written

Yes I'm Ready with E.S. McMillan

For What It's Worth with E.S. McMillan
Cherry Poppin Blast with Leah Negron
Wax Me with Pleasure with Michael S Mann
Cuffed For Pleasure with Michael S. Mann
Purgatory's Apostle with Steven Evans

Crowns Of Chaos MC

Prince In The Big Apple
Rough In The Big Apple
Cappy In The Big Apple

Michael s. Mann

Wax Me with Pleasure with JA Lafrance
Cuffed For Pleasure with JA Lafrance
Love, Death and Life After

Contact the authors

JA Lafrance

Http://jalafrance.wixsite.com/website[1]

Michael Mann

https://www.facebook.com/michaelsmannauthor/

https://www.bookbub.com/profile/michael-mann-51a43a84-bec4-4957-b987-854d1ec55834?list=author_books

---